"SECRET ASSIGNMENTS"

A Humorous Look at a Dangerous Job!

By

KEVIN R. ILLIA

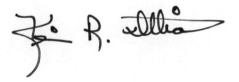

ISBN: 1-4107-3262-2 (e-book)
ISBN: 1-4107-3263-0 (Paperback)
ISBN: 1-4107-3264-9 (Dust Jacket)

Library of Congress Control Number: 2003092418

This book is printed on acid free paper.

Printed in the United States of America
Bloomington, IN

1stBooks - rev. 05/16/03

A special thanks to the outstanding efforts of Marilyn Peck, without whose patience and organizational skills this manuscript would not be possible.

Lastly, to the men and women of the FBI who go out daily about the people's business and place themselves in harm's way so that America can remain the land of the free and the home of the brave. And, the man who leads this incredibly talented group of people, Robert S. Mueller III, Director of the world's greatest investigative agency.

I thank all of you for your support and friendship.

Kevin Illia

Chicago, Illinois

FOREWORD

The impetus for this book came from not only my family but from the lack of current books regarding the exploits of FBI Agents in today's society.

I decided to write a book which reflected the humorous side of the serious business of crime with the hope it would entertain the public and also inspire young people to want to enter government service. The ability to recruit outstanding candidates for government service depends not only on the job being available but also on information which will motivate young people to want to serve this nation.

It is with these two goals in mind that I have set forth the adventures of Agent Man and his Secret Assignments.

I would also like to thank my colleagues in this book—such legendary Special Agents as Pete Wacks, his brother Mike Wacks, George Mandich, Dick Herman, Phil Grivas, Tom Flynn, Parnell Miles, Jim Brown, Jim Newcomb, Paula Brand, Mike Pavia, Marie Dyson, Gary Kissinger, Ernie Luera and so many others—for their support in this effort.

CHAPTER ONE

A ROOKIE IN WASHINGTON, D.C.

The Nation's Capitol

Washington, D.C.

The air was crisp as a new day began to dawn in Chicago. We were surveilling the El Borracho Tavern on the southwest side of the city in an area called "El Pueblito."

Special Agent Peter "The Professor" Wacks was my partner and we were accompanied by Chicago FBI SWAT Commander Tony "The Tiger" Savarese and his ninja warriors.

Tony turned and spoke quietly, "Agent Man, it's 0600 and show time." I turned to Peter, "Professor, are we ready to strike a blow against narcotics traffickers?" "I believe we are," replied Pete as he raised his baby sledgehammer, "Let's get it on!"

Tony got on the radio and with military precision the agents took up their pre-planned positions around the tavern to abort any escape attempts.

Pete, Tony and I, along with four of our young agents, crossed the street, announced our presence, and pounded on the door. Our objective was Carlos Antonio Fuentes, a member of the Juarez drug cartel and a main distributor of cocaine among the Hispanic population in Chicago.

A light went on upstairs and a woman came down to the door which had a glass window. I shouted, "FBI! Open the door!" She shrugged and replied, "No entiendo!" I repeated, "FBI! Abra la puerta!" At that point Pete raised the sledgehammer. The door immediately opened. "See, she doesn't speak Spanish, she speaks sledgehammer," Peter shouted as we raced up the stairs.

While Tony's SWAT team was securing the inside of the tavern and conducting a search of the premises, we quickly reached the second floor and checked the bedrooms, which were empty. We then heard shouting down the narrow hallway. We ran down the hallway with our automatics leading the way. The passage led to a stairway and racing up toward us were two black-clad ninja warriors with submachine guns in hand. In large white letters across their chests were the initials "FBI." "Oh, it's the good guys," quipped Pete. The agents advised that the subject had been hiding in the tavern and escaped up a back staircase.

We quickly located the continuation of the staircase hidden behind cardboard boxes. The stairs led to a trapdoor up to the roof. As I reached the roof the sunrise silhouetted the outline of a man poised at the roof's edge.

I yelled, "Carlos! FBI. It's over!" Two young agents were immediately on either side of me with their MP-3 submachine guns trained on the subject. The silence was broken as Pete emerged from the trapdoor and announced, "I'm getting too old for this shit." "I agree, partner," I answered.

Carlos then spoke. "Don't come any closer or I'll jump." We were frozen in place. Without replying to Carlos, I spoke. "Professor, it appears we have a problem." "Yes, we do," said Pete, "But, there are options so why don't you explain them to Carlos, Agent Man."

"Okay now, Carlos, this is a bad situation but let me explain it to you. It isn't the end of the world unless, of course, you jump. I'd say you probably have a family that loves you. They're probably Catholic and in the Catholic Church suicide is a sin. More importantly, is a little time in the joint worth killing yourself over? We have a few more arrests to make this morning, so here's the deal. The gentlemen dressed in black next to me are expert marksmen and will shoot you if you desire. Or, you can break your family's hearts by jumping. Or you can do the smart thing and climb down off the ledge, let us take you into custody and lunch is on us. What do you say, Carlos? Option number three?"

A very long moment went by as we all stared at Carlos. He looked down for a few seconds and then climbed off the ledge. The young agents ran over, patted him down, and cuffed him behind his back. As they took him away, he commented, "Man, you really are full of bullshit." "Yes, he is," Pete agreed and started to laugh. I grinned and said, "Well, he didn't get a chance to hear you speak or he would have known there were two of us!" Pete laughed again and said he was going to call in the apprehension and check in with Tony, the SWAT commander, to see if we had any other unfamiliar faces in all the wrong places. I told him that was a good idea and I would be along shortly.

As I stood on the roof and looked back toward downtown Chicago, skyscrapers outlined against a beautiful sunrise, I thought of my first months in the FBI in the early 1970's...

I had grown up in San Francisco, graduated from high school there, and then joined the United States Air Force. I had served a combat tour in Vietnam in the 1960's and had returned to go to college at the height of the anti-war movement. Since I was a combat veteran attending college, I was viewed as an aberration. The pursuit of a higher education was cloaked in the political rhetoric of the time. Being who I am, I have never been considered politically correct in any decade, but people always knew where I stood on the pressing issues of the day.

I received an appointment as a Special Agent of the FBI on February 8, 1971, in a letter signed by the legendary FBI Director J. Edgar Hoover. A lot of negative comments and allegations have been written about Mr. Hoover, but I was very proud to have served under his leadership. He was very firm but fair and initiated the changes in the FBI that made it the premier investigative agency in the world. The present Director, Robert S. Mueller III, has continued to promote the creative innovations in investigative techniques which have

5

propelled the FBI beyond any other law enforcement agency in the world, such as New Scotland Yard or the Royal Canadian Mounted Police. Mr. Mueller has obtained funding for software information systems and DNA research which have revolutionized information management during investigations and the ability to identify subjects of previously unsolved crimes due to breakthroughs in DNA science.

My arrival in Washington, D.C., in the early 1970's was marked by a flooded shower and room at the Harrington Hotel in downtown Washington. The FBI Academy of today on the grounds of the U.S. Marine Base at Quantico, Virginia, had not been completed at the time I entered the service.

Then, new agents' training was held at both the Old Post Office Building on Pennsylvania Avenue (now a shopping mall) and a two-story barracks building on the Marine base at Quantico. The barracks building is now an administrative annex building utilized by the Marine Corps.

We were given our orientation briefing by the Assistant Director of the FBI, "Jumping Joe" Casper, who lived up to his reputation. As we sat in our starched white shirts, dark suits and conservative ties (no blue shirts or yellow ties permitted), Mr. Casper paced the stage of the Department of Justice auditorium like a caged lion ready to pounce.

He reminded all of us how lucky we were to have received our appointments, how Mr. Hoover had spent a lifetime building the reputation of the FBI, and that no one in the room should ever embarrass the Bureau or his career would be over. Lastly, he pointed out that the American public had entrusted FBI agents with enforcing the law of the land and no one was above that law, including all of us sitting in front of him.

By the end of Mr. Casper's presentation we were all intimidated, not knowing if we had been hired or fired.

Fortunately, the next Bureau official to speak was quite a bit less dramatic, actually stood at the podium, and was soft-spoken. He discussed the administrative details of our schedules, class subjects and hours, and what was expected of each new agent during the training process.

There was a mutual sigh of relief as we realized we still had jobs.

Since the course lasted three months, temporary housing was needed and I hooked up with two of my classmates, Pete Flanagan and Steve "Handcuffs" Hummel, to rent rooms at a boarding house behind the nation's capitol. The rooms were reasonable, clean and within walking distance of the Old Post Office.

We took classes in communications, report writing, court proceedings, the FBI's organizational structure, and federal law. The highlight of my day was one hour of physical defense tactics held in the basement gym of the Department of Justice.

After two months of training, including Saturday morning classes, we departed by bus to the U.S. Marine Base and the two-story building leased by the FBI for firearms training. I have never talked to a FBI Special Agent who did not enjoy this part of the curriculum. The course did not consist of just weapon safety. We were given exposure to weapons used by foreign governments and a general crash course in all types of firearms and how they function.

The on-line firearms training was then and remains some of the best in the world. Mr. Hoover insisted that his agents be able to shoot faster and more accurately then the criminals who chose to engage them. After hours and hours on the range I actually felt that my pistol was an extension of my body.

There were times over the next quarter of a century when I had to draw my sidearm but I knew that because of the reputation of FBI

Agents as expert shots the offenders often laid down their weapon rather that test the theory.

After three intense weeks at the Marine Base, we headed back to Washington to receive our assignments in field offices around the nation. The assignments are made based on the specific needs of the Bureau. It is an exciting time for a new agent because the field is where the crimes are solved and the action takes place.

Things had gone well with our New Agents' Class. We had started with thirty-two candidates and had lost only two who had dropped out of training for family reasons.

On my first Monday back in Washington, I walked out onto the steps of the boardinghouse and a small white petal fluttered down onto my suit coat. It was from a cherry blossom. I looked up and down the street and saw that all of the cherry trees were in bloom. Across the street was the Supreme Court building and as I walked further down the street the Capitol Building emerged before my eyes. I had taken an oath to defend the country and on this particular day the country looked pretty nice to me, especially Washington D.C. in the springtime.

Kevin R. Illia

My mood was upbeat until I passed the Capitol Building and saw that thousands of anti-war demonstrators had come to town to shut down the government. The lawns of the capitol were filled with the Metro Police Department's finest, arranged in twenty-man units on Vespa scooters, their shiny powder blue helmets reflecting the sun. The scene reminded me of the Roman legions ready for battle and waiting for the orders to engage. They did not have to wait long.

As I proceeded into the fray, I could observe demonstrators picking up four-by-four logs, similar to railroad ties, and heaving them onto cars stopped for a traffic light. I heard the sirens and didn't have to turn around to know that the legions had been launched. As they approached, the demonstrators retreated from a construction site which had been the source of their logs.

The scene was getting ugly and I knew I looked totally out of place with my suit and briefcase. I continued down Pennsylvania Avenue to the Department of Justice Building just in time to watch demonstrators surround the building and declare the government shut down. This presented a big problem because Mr. Hoover expected us all to show up.

As I viewed the scene I decided to start off nice because everyone likes nice. I approached a tall slender male with long hair and round glasses on his nose. He wore a black turtleneck sweater and Levi's.

"Excuse me, I need to get into that building," I said. The young man looked at me in disgust and sneered, "I'm afraid the building's shut down and nobody's getting in there!"

"Well, you see, I work there. I'm a new employee and respect your right to protest the war, but I hoped you'd respect my right to go to work."

"Look," the bespectacled man argued, "The reason we're here is that neo-facist people like you screwed up the country and got us into an immoral war!"

It was quite evident to me that things were not progressing well and the conversation was deteriorating rapidly.

"You know, I've tried to be understanding. I've even acknowledged your right to be here." Then I leaned over and whispered in the young man's ear, "Look, motherfucker, underneath this coat is a fifteen-shot automatic that I'm going to ram down your crotch and terminate your personal protest. Now, get out of my way or I'll terminate you!" His eyes got wide, his expression was of

11

disbelief and the demonstrator stepped aside. I smiled as I passed by and said, "Have a nice day."

When I arrived upstairs, the class counselor looked at me and asked if there was any problem getting into the building. "No, sir. Just a little confusion as to where to access the line but everyone was very cooperative once I explained my position." The counselor, being an inquisitive FBI man, looked puzzled and asked, "Now, what position would that be?" "I'm armed," I answered. "Oh, yeah. That's always a good position," he grinned.

The week went by quickly as all Special Agent training does, filled with a million things to accomplish in a very short time. Finally the big day arrived and I learned my first assignment would be to the FBI's field office in Detroit, Michigan. I was excited = Motown, the Supremes, General Motors, and, at that time, Detroit was the homicide capital of the world, having surpassed New York City the year before. A dubious honor, but for a new Special Agent, being where the action was would be a great learning experience. I would fly that Friday, after classes had ended, directly to Detroit, not taking any leave in order to start my new life.

…"What are you thinking about?" I heard a voice call out. My concentration broken, I turned to see "The Professor" standing on the roof behind me. "I was just thinking back a quarter of a century when I started in this business," I replied.

Pete smiled and then asked, "Was that before or after Custer's Last Stand?" "You know what's really great about this job? You get a damn good partner plus a standup comedian along with it."

"Well, I'm glad you're in a good mood because we've got a hostage situation on Archer Avenue and our presence has been requested. Obviously not for our physical prowess but for our experience," Pete continued.

"Professor, the beat goes on so let's get over there and see what this whacko wants!"

"Just remember, Agent Man, we have a lot of options available to us in dealing with this poor outcast," Pete remarked.

"If I wanted options, I'd go to the Chicago Board of Trade. Let's get these people out of harm's way," I said.

As Pete started down through the trapdoor he stopped and observed, "It's a great job and a great career, isn't it?"

"Yes, it's the best job in America," I agreed.

CHAPTER TWO

MOTOWN: CARS ARE THE STARS

Detroit,

Michigan

As the taxi arrived in front of the Albert Pick Hotel in downtown Detroit, I realized I had finally made it to Motown, the home of Berry Gordy and the Supremes. All the groups I had grown up with had their origins here. Now, Motown was going to have assigned to it the world's greatest secret agent, ready to take back the streets, reverse its reputation as the Murder Capital of the country, and return to the sounds of the Sixties.

My high expectations were immediately tested after I paid the cab driver. A vendor of "gold" jewelry came up to me and asked if I would be interested in a twenty-four- carat gold watch or necklace for the "little lady." Since I had a watch but no "little lady" or even a "big lady", the answer was "No."

"By the way, do you have a vendor's license to sell in front of the hotel?" His reply was, "No, and you're not a tourist, are you?" I counseled the man about selling in the street after eight p.m. and then noticed that what he was selling was not gold. The man laughed and then said, "I could have just robbed you." I replied, "Precisely the reason I'm here, my good fellow, and why you will now cease and desist until you go to city hall for a vendor's license." He picked up his suitcase and left.

The Albert Pick had seen better days but belonging to the most frugal government agency in the nation, I was well schooled in Mr. Hoover's philosophy of getting more bang for the buck when spending the taxpayer's money. The term "first class" was not included in the Bureau's lexicon, and, when it came to agent accommodations, the cheaper the better. When you submitted your travel voucher, headquarters would try to screw you out of even that amount. The agents, being resourceful in addition to being faithful, brave and loyal, would find a way to get reimbursed.

I checked into my substandard room, hung up my suit for the following day, and cleaned my pistol before retiring for the evening.

My new assignment was to a criminal squad that consisted of fifteen Special Agents whose investigations concerned interstate auto theft, escaped federal prisoners and, at that time, military deserters.

The one thing in Detroit bigger than the rock 'n' roll groups was the manufacturing of automobiles, followed by the theft and shipment all over the world of stolen vehicles.

During my first week on the squad, I teamed up with Agent Mike Staulder, who was about six feet four inches and had played football in the Big Ten. He would later leave the FBI and become a successful real estate developer in Florida. Mike was the man who handled the auto theft ring investigations and was well along the way to cracking one, operating out of the General Motors Plant in Hamtramck, Michigan, when I arrived.

At the time, General Motors was manufacturing Buicks and Chevies at the plant. The new vehicles were stored in huge parking lots surrounding the plant. The vehicle identification number was not assigned to the vehicle until after the car left the premises. This procedure would change at a later date and after much correspondence, including Director Hoover's correspondence with the

President of General Motors. When Mr. Hoover contacted anyone it was a pretty good bet that he would get their immediate attention.

Clearly, the vehicles sitting in the parking lots were ripe for theft, as any half-ass theft ring could fabricate or, in our case, steal the identification numbers prior to the manufacturer's issuing an assigned number. Mike Staulder had identified a subject who was stealing the numbers and who was related by marriage to the parking lot supervisor.

Now, to give you an idea of the enormity of this theft ring, most rows of new cars contained twenty vehicles. The parking personnel would inventory the cars each morning by row. The attendant would count, "I have Row 48, 49, 51," and so on. The only trouble was the entire Row 50 was missing.

We had identified the two relatives, and a credit check quickly revealed they were living above their salaries. The Internal Revenue Service was kind enough to verify that they had no other declared sources of income. Since people do not list illegal sources of income, we decided to concentrate on the two in-laws, or, in this case, out-laws. The phone records of both showed several calls between them on the dates of the thefts, as well as to an unidentified phone number.

17

By the time I arrived there had been four incidents of theft involving almost one hundred cars. We determined the unidentified telephone number was listed to a woman who worked as a secretary in a downtown bank. A discreet investigation of the woman revealed that while the phone number was listed in her name, she leased her apartment to a Mr. and Mrs. Kendall.

Mr. Kendall turned out to be David Kendall whose employment with the Argus Security Service put him on the midnight shift in, of all places, the parking lot at the Hamtramck General Motors plant.

We had the players but did not have the script explaining how the cars left the plant and disappeared into the night. We knew that the thefts occurred during the third or fourth week of the month and usually on a Thursday or Friday evening. We decided to set up a physical surveillance and observe the midnight activity at the plant.

On the last Saturday of the month, about 3:00 a.m., two eight-bed car-carriers pulled into the parking lot and, after a short conversation with the security guard, the drivers loaded sixteen cars. It all seemed so normal that no one paid any attention to the activity, except for the ten Special Agents of the FBI whose radios suddenly came alive.

The decision was made to follow the car-carriers. Their destination was a warehouse on the East Side of Detroit near the Detroit River. The drivers turned out to be the relatives. After they unloaded the cars and left, we found a window and, using flashlights, were not surprised to see the entire floor of the warehouse taken up by brand new Buicks and Chevies.

The warehouse was not owned by General Motors but by a shipping company who had leased it to one of the relatives.

The U.S. Attorney's Office in Detroit was excited and pressed for arrest warrants in addition to search warrants.

The arrest of the auto theft ring and, subsequently, the arrests of those individuals who had been receiving the stolen vehicles culminated in the conviction of twenty-two individuals and the seizure of over two million dollars worth of stolen cars. After all, in Detroit the cars are the stars.

Our boss was so happy about the success of the investigation that he recommended we each be awarded $100.00 incentive awards, which we received. Actually, it was $75.00 for each of us because $25.00 was taken out for Uncle Sam.

Needless to say, this case improved our working relationship with the executives at General Motors and this helped me a great deal.

I had inherited an "old dog" case from a retiring agent. It concerned an escaped federal prisoner who had long ago disappeared. He had escaped from a minimum security work crew at the penitentiary in Atlanta, Georgia. The fugitive had sold shares in a floral company to members of the black community in and around Atlanta. The idea was to rent out plastic flowers for funerals. He realized that his market niche was in the poorer neighborhoods and the plastic flowers would afford the deceased a decent burial. The shareholders' pocketbooks would benefit because the plastic flowers could be rented out over and over again.

As bizarre as it sounds, people could understand the idea, were counting the dollars that would be coming in, and enthusiastically invested. The fugitive had raised $260,000 before someone checked. There was no floral company and the investors' money was in another state.

I had an eight-year-old photo of a handsome black man, now thirty-five years old, who had vanished. The man had been born and raised in Detroit before moving to Atlanta. I went back to the old neighborhood and interviewed friends and neighbors. The consensus was that he had died or started a new life. The interesting thing I found was that no one referred to him as Reginald Lewis Lampkins. Everyone called him "Rickey," yet no one seemed to know where that name came from. The FBI file I had reviewed always referred to him as Reginald Lampkins, as did all official documents. I thought, "If I know this, then Rickey knows it, too."

I began to do some background checks on the name Rickey or Richard L. Lampkins. It should not have come as a complete surprise when I came up with twenty-seven Rickey Lampkins living in and around Detroit. Luckily, I had the birth date of my Rickey, which pared the number down to five possibilities. I worked down the list to number three. A credit check indicated he had lived in the area for the past seven years, had married, had purchased a home and was an executive trainee in the General Motors program to promote qualified minority candidates. The report showed that Mr. Lampkins was presently working at the General Motors Plant in Hamtramck, Michigan. Since I already knew my way to that plant, I gathered three other agents and headed out.

We were warmly greeted at the plant manager's office since our auto theft ring arrests were still being talked about there. We sat down with the manager and told him about our investigation. It was as if a lightning bolt had struck him. He was sure we had the wrong man because he thought of his employee as an outstanding role model whom he had personally mentored and he was very proud of the man's achievements.

I asked to see the personnel file and the manager went to get it. I told the other agents there should be a photo in it which would settle the matter.

As I opened the file, I knew everything was coming up roses. The plant manager called in Rickey Lampkins. I introduced myself, "Mr. Lampkins, we aren't from the FTD. We're from the FBI." Rickey sank into the chair and looked at me. "You wouldn't consider a pass, would you? I'm really doing well at this place." I answered, "I'm afraid that's not possible."

The plant manager stared in disbelief as we cuffed Mr. Lampkins.

At the FBI Office, Reginald Lampkins related the story of a Georgia rain storm, the guards had all taken cover under a bridge, leaving the prisoners unattended. He took it as a sign from God and left. He returned to Detroit, got a job, found a girl, and then enrolled in the General Motors program. When I inquired about how he got his college degree, he said he "created the documentation" and it had been accepted. He decided to apply for his driver's license as Rickey Lampkins since everyone called him by that name anyway and he did not want to deal with a false name as it usually trips you up in the end.

Rickey Lampkins was sorry for having defrauded the investors. Because of his new life and excellent work record at General Motors, he would get a reduced sentence with court supervision, and go on to become a productive citizen.

CHAPTER THREE

THE STRAWBERRY KING GOES BANANAS

St. Joseph,

Michigan

The southwest portion of the Great State of Michigan lies within one of the great fruit-growing regions of the United States. While still known for its automobile production and supporting industries, Michigan has had a healthy fruit-growing history. In and around St. Joseph, Michigan, cherries, peaches, cantaloupes and corn have been grown for years. Increasing grape production and a prosperous wine industry have been consuming acreage for the past several years. Like all businesses that produce products or crops, there is money to be made.

Early in my FBI career, I was assigned to a resident agency in this area. The resident agency was composed of two Special Agents beside myself—the Senior Resident Agent, one of my early mentors,

Leo K. "Pat" Cook, and his assistant whom he had recruited twenty-four years before, the nervous but gentle John Sullivan. Pat Cook was brilliant, had graduated from the University of Notre Dame, finished law school, served as a Special Agent in Chicago, and, because of his long association with Director J. Edgar Hoover, had gotten the "Old Man" to approve a transfer back home. Pat Cook represented all that was great about the FBI and was the epitome of what a Special Agent should stand for in the profession. He was also an outstanding investigator who knew his territory and everyone in it, and could usually outguess the criminals after they committed the crime but before they effected an escape.

The other member of our agent trio was John Sullivan, a fine family man who pursued the inventing of board games which he hoped Parker Brothers would choose to sell and he would retire a wealthy man. John, like Pat, had been born and raised in Southwestern Michigan and it was through Pat's intervention that John Sullivan ended up as his assistant in the resident agency.

I was very lucky to have started my career with such resourceful agents. I had come to the area from the Detroit Office of the FBI, where I had worked on an auto theft squad. In the City of Detroit that

25

Kevin R. Illia

was a full-time job. Not only were more cars manufactured there but more cars were stolen there.

I was the junior man in the office and pulled a lot of weekend standby duty. Since I was new, it actually helped me to meet the law enforcement people in the three counties our territory encompassed. The FBI maintains field offices, or divisions, in cities throughout the United States. It is within these divisions that smaller satellite offices, called resident agencies, exist. The size of the resident agency is usually determined by population and criminal activity in the respective area.

The fruit belt of Southwestern Michigan was not the center of crime in the state but like any area of the country had enough dishonest people to keep us gainfully employed.

While I had chased federal fugitives through the cantaloupe fields of Michigan, which is no easy feat in a suit, I had also arrested my first escaped federal prisoner picking apples in a tree. I believe my statement to him ran something like, "Hi, I'm with the FBI and I think you know why I'm here. Would you like to come down or do I need to come up?" His surprised reply was, "Apple?"

We had received a phone call from a strawberry farmer named John Provolone who, it turned out, was the "Strawberry King" of Southwestern Michigan. It seems he had consigned $20,000 worth of strawberries of Kempf Brothers Trucking Company for delivery to the market in Chicago. The strawberries never made it and the Kempf brothers were nowhere to be found.

I drove north one morning from St. Joseph, Michigan, across the bridge spanning the St. Joseph River, north along the eastern shore of Lake Michigan on Highway 31, until I arrived at the Provolone Farm. I drove in on the gravel road to a large brownish brick residence. It was very quiet. A blue Ford pickup was parked in the driveway near a white barn with a red shingled roof. As I walked up the steps to ring the bell, the door flew open and a short white man with a black baseball cap and a mask on his face stood in front of me.

My first thought was "home invasion in progress!" I immediately went into my stance, my .38 caliber Smith & Wesson had cleared leather, and, before I could think, the words came tumbling out, "FBI. Freeze!" The man froze in shock. I grabbed him as h e was trying to talk and shoved him against the outside wall. "Okay, spread 'em wide, little guy. This party is over," I exclaimed. The man did what he was

27

told. As I was speaking, I noticed the shadow of someone else to my left. I turned, weapon in hand, to meet the second perpetrator and was met with a most unusual sight—a heavy, rotund woman in a kitchen smock of blue, dotted with white lilies. Her eyes were wide, her mouth open, as she bellowed, "What are you doing and who are you?"

I replied instantly, "Special Agent Kevin Illia, FBI, Ma'am. Nothing to worry about. Are there other perpetrators inside?" She looked at me incredulously and answered, "No, sir. And neither is my husband who you have up against the wall!"

There are times when that sinking feeling overcomes you, realizing that you have totally misjudged a situation. This was one of those times. It is during those moments that diplomacy and professionalism must come to the forefront to alleviate the dilemma.

The first thing was to holster the weapon. Done! Then, take the owner off the wall. Done!

In my most contrite voice, I asked, "So…Mr. Provolone, what's with the mask? In Detroit, where I was recently assigned, it usually means robbery in progress."

For the first time, the Strawberry King spoke. "I suffer from asthma and high blood pressure. Excuse me while I get my pills." "Sure, no problem," I replied.

"Mrs. Provolone, I'm here about the missing strawberries." Mrs. Provolone then invited me in, as long as the gun stayed holstered. Again, I apologized profusely and said that in my business one does not always get a second chance.

Mrs. Provolone parked me in the living room on a green couch which was brand new, or at least it gave that appearance, and encased in plastic. There was a lovely glass table with a plastic flower arrangement and end chairs which matched the couch, also still covered in plastic.

Mrs. Provolone returned with some invoices in hand and explained that her husband had bid out to the lowest bidder, Kempf Brothers Trucking Company, a shipment of 10,000 pounds of strawberries, valued at $20,000, to be transported from Michigan to the Water Street Fruit Market in Chicago, Illinois.

One day after this shipment left his farm, Mr. Provolone received a call from Bob Kempf, the driver and principal owner of the trucking company, who told him that the truck had broken down near Gary,

Indiana, the refrigeration had gone down, and the strawberries had rotted on the shoulder of Interstate Highway 94. Mr. Kempf had indicated he would send a copy of the police report for insurance purposes and was truly sorry.

At this point, Mr. Provolone got red in the face, eyes bulging, becoming more and more agitated, until he just "went bananas." He angrily recounted how a friend of his, Gino Testa, a fruit wholesaler in Detroit, had called him a few days after the truck breakdown and said Bob and Bill Kempf had arrived at the fruit market in Detroit and sold 10,000 pounds of strawberries at below market value in a cash-and-carry transaction. Mr. Testa had gone on to say that the boxes bore the imprint of "Provolone Farms, Berrien County, Michigan."

As I calmed Mr. Provolone down, he recalled how he had attempted to call Kempf Trucking Company but the line had been disconnected and the address turned out to be a vacant lot in Hobart, Indiana.

The case that had started out as a joke appeared to have enough life to it to merit a possible violation of the Interstate Transportation of Stolen Property statute or, in the parlance of the FBI, and ITSP violation with merit.

The United States Attorney's Office for the Western District of Michigan was located in Grand Rapids about eighty miles from our office in Benton Harbor. I called and made an appointment to see Assistant U.S. Attorney Bob Green.

Bob was one of the great career government attorneys that I would have the pleasure of working with during my career in the FBI. He was knowledgeable, professional and, most importantly, a great listener. We had worked on other criminal matters so we had already established a track record. One of the most admirable qualities that I sought out from Assistant U.S. Attorneys was a sense of humor about the work we did. There are a lot of frustrations, obstacles and distractions before a case goes to trial and a conviction is obtained. It takes people who are willing to go the distance and overcome those barriers if one is to be successful. Many of the people involved in the criminal justice system are neither ready nor equipped to make that type of commitment. A sense of humor smoothes out the rough spots.

As I walked into Bob's office, I realized he was harassed, buried in reviewing cases, and preparing for trial. "Bob, buddy, I have a very unusual case for you," I exclaimed, trying my best to "sell" the case.

Bob smiled at me and said, "I'm listening!" I then launched into the facts surrounding the missing strawberries and before I could get far Bob burst out laughing. "This is a joke, right? Kevin, I love it when you come into my office. It's like the free entertainment that I miss out on at night because I'm always here." I stopped and smiled, "Not exactly. Bob, this really happened. The strawberries are gone, the truckers are gone, the money's gone. The value is well over $5,000 and those little strawberries tippy-toed across state lines into the Hoosier State of Indiana."

"God, you're serious," Bob replied as he straightened up in his chair and began to grasp the case. For a few seconds he sat there staring at the wall and then responded, "Stolen strawberries across state lines. Screw it, let's go get them!"

"You realize that you'll be branded a rogue assistant, just like I'm branded a rogue agent," I pointed out. "Yeah," he said, "That's okay. So, what else is new?"

Having the backing of the U. S. Attorney's Office was important before I expended a lot of time working up the case.

"The King" had kept copious notes and, with the permission of the FBI in Indiana, I traveled to the Indiana State Police Post in Gary. The desk sergeant called in the trooper who had worked that shift on the date of the alleged breakdown. We went back in the records room and in the efficient fashion of the Indiana State Police he quickly pulled out his report on the Kempf eighteen-wheeler. I interviewed him regarding the incident and everything checked out until, almost jokingly, I asked what you did with 10,000 pounds of rotten strawberries since this had not been included in the report. The trooper stated that Bob Kempf was lucky because his brother, Bill Kempf, just happened to be returning empty in a refrigerated truck from the market in Chicago.

"Wow, what a break! So, let me guess. The strawberries were not rotten but were transferred in perfect condition to the other truck?" I asked. The trooper responded, "Yes, sir. I stayed until the shipment was transferred and the tow truck arrived."

This was the first crack in the dam, but a long way from a raging river. I still had a lot of work to do. Two other cases also demanded my time: One a bank robbery that was quickly solved as the robber wrote the demand note on the back of a deposit slip which contained her home address. And two, a kidnapping, the victim of which was found deposited in our territory. The victim had been abducted by two

33

parking attendants from Milwaukee, Wisconsin, who were subsequently charged, not as you might think, for trying to accomplish the longest valet parking job in history (three states away), but, rather, for abducting the owner with her car. These two cases completed, I returned to the case of the missing strawberries.

Three weeks had passed and the "Strawberry King" began calling twice a week for a progress report. He was not in a good mood and had trouble accepting the fact that federal cases take time.

Gino Testa, the fruit vendor from Detroit, proved to be a compelling witness who not only retained one of the cases marked "Provolone Farms, Berrien County, Michigan," but also furnished the names of four others at the market who had witnessed the Kempfs unload and sell the strawberries.

The address on the original transport invoice turned out to be a piece of property owned by a cousin of the Kempfs who indicated the brothers had been in trouble with the law before. A check of the Michigan State Police criminal files produced two lovely mug shots of the Brothers Kempf. After a return trip to Detroit and a photo display with Gino Testa & Company, the two brothers were positively identified as having unloaded the shipment.

Ten months after Mr. Provolone's phone call to the FBI, at a '76 Truck Stop near New Buffalo, Michigan, accompanied by Special Agents Pat Cook and John Sullivan and two Michigan state troopers, I sat down at the breakfast counter with Bill and Bob Kempf.

"Good morning, boys," I greeted them. "How are those waffles? Good, I hope. The only thing that would make them better would be some strawberries.

Bob Kempf looked at me and said, "This isn't going to be good, is it?" I answered, "No, boys, it's not."

Bob Green looked at me after we left the courtroom and the judge had accepted the guilty pleas for the interstate transportation of stolen strawberries, and said, "You realize you're a folk hero now to twenty-thousand Michigan fruit farmers, don't you?" I grinned, "Oh, come on, you're making me blush!"

The Kempf brothers would serve three years each in a federal prison and have their Michigan truckers' licenses revoked forever.

The "Strawberry King" stopped calling and was once again happy after the court awarded him $35,000 from the forfeiture sale of the trucking company. I happily moved on to my next case.

CHAPTER FOUR

THE FREIGHT AND JUNK SQUAD

St. Louis,

Missouri

The St. Louis Arch has often been compared to a giant McDonald's Hamburger symbol rising over the mighty Mississippi River. The city itself was founded by French fur traders and evolved into one of the solid Midwestern towns that make America great.

In August, 1972, I was assigned to the FBI Division in St. Louis and had the opportunity to work with some very gifted investigators, both in the St. Louis Police Department and in the FBI. Unlike Detroit, the St. Louis FBI and the local police enjoyed a close relationship of mutual cooperation. Because of that we were a lot more successful in detecting, investigating and preventing criminal groups from operating for any length of time. One of the very sharp police detectives that I worked with was Clarence Harmon. Not only was Clarence very capable but he had a great sense of humor. Clarence would go on to become the Chief of Police and the first African-American Mayor of St. Louis. I have always been proud of our friendship. Clarence Harmon put his family and his community first in spite of a lot of obstacles which would have precluded a less determined individual from accomplishing his goals.

There was another small group of investigators with whom I worked in the St. Louis Police Department that handled cases no one else in the police department would take on.

My introduction to this group was made by my fellow agent and life-long friend, Special Agent Dick Herman. Dick and I went to police headquarters one morning to gather background information concerning a series of thefts of government office equipment from several federal buildings in and around the St. Louis metropolitan area.

We went to the fourth floor of police headquarters, walked down a dark corridor, turned left past two small offices and up to a wooden door. The door had a glass pane with gold letters—"Freight and Junk Squad." It was a scene out of the 1920's and I just started laughing.

I said, "Dick, does the rest of the police department even know this place exists?" "Oh, yeah!" Dick answered, "These guys are for real!" If you knew Dick Herman you realized how enthusiastic he was about everything and everyone. In all the years I have known him I have never heard him speak ill of anyone.

We walked through the door to a wooden counter. Sitting at a wooden desk behind the counter with a cigar in his mouth, leaning back in a chair with his black cowboy boots resting on the desk, was the legendary Sgt. "Boots" Lewellyn of the St. Louis Police Department. Boots was assisted in his battle against crime by Detective Jim Breshnan and Sgt. Herman Ubben, about whom it was rumored that he had escaped from an asylum and was being hidden out at Freight and Junk by Boots. This rumor started because Sgt. Ubben liked to be called "Herman the German" and would volunteer for any dangerous assignment. I would learn that all of this made sense as I began to work with this crew in solving the crimes no one else wanted. People could call them crazy but this eccentric group got results, solved crimes, put people in jail and recovered property. It was also a very closed group that did not accept just anyone at face value.

Agent Dick Herman (no relation to "Herman the German") greased the wheels for me when, after introducing me, stated, "He's O.K.!" It was with these words that I was accepted completely into the Freight and Junk Squad as an honorary member attached to, as Boots liked to say, the "Federal Freight and Junk Liaison Group."

Since Boots and the boys did this every day, their advice was welcomed. We provided the dates of thefts, serial numbers and descriptions of the stolen government equipment, the value of which was quickly approaching $150,000. Our Special Agent in Charge wanted the case solved as he was receiving calls from government building managers who were hearing from the "victim" government agency heads regarding the thefts.

Since we had no suspects and everyone was in agreement that the private security force or the night cleaning crew were probably involved, we needed to know who was working the nights of the thefts and determine if there was any correlation. Dick and I accepted that assignment since most of the employees were on contract to the federal government.

Herman the German and Jim Breshnan, at Boots' *suggestion* (never an *order*, which I loved) would cover their informants and also the "fences" in the city.

A "fence" is a criminal (of course, he would say he's a businessman), who receives stolen property at anywhere from twenty-five to forty percent of the actual value. He then sells it at a "front" store, or to another individual, with a markup large enough that he would accept the risk but still below the true market value, thereby translating into a "deal" for the customer.

The Freight and Junk Squad had arrested several fences over the years and, like all good street officers, continued to check on them and receive information from them.

After a few weeks we sat down to compare information and determine in which direction the investigation was headed. Dick and I had drawn a blank on the contract employees and the security guards. Detective Jim Breshnan had developed information regarding a new guy on the west side who was offering merchandise, mainly office equipment, to be established criminal fences.

Since we were not getting anywhere doing background investigations, Boots suggested we approach the problem from the "other end" and try a reverse sting operation.

The idea sounded good but I wondered how we would proceed. Boots explained we would put an undercover agent into the market and see if he would be able to "inspect" the merchandise before he bought it. If the serial numbers on the merchandise matched the serial numbers on our inventory of stolen items we would be on the right track. As soon as Boots mentioned using an undercover agent, Herman the German jumped up from his seat and yelled, "I'm your man. Send me in, Coach!"

We all stared at Herman. Boots then spoke. "Sit down, you fuckin' nut case." Herman quietly sat down and did not utter another word during the entire meeting.

We arranged a plan of action which called for Jim Breshnan to have his criminal source introduce Herman as the owner of a secondhand store on Manchester Road that specialized in used office equipment. The rest of us would set up a physical surveillance of Herman, who would be wired for sound and have a small walkie-talkie sequestered in his truck.

Kevin R. Illia

The subject of the case was a Peter Castellas who, it turns out, was employed by a legitimate office products company. He was a technician who regularly visited federal offices to work on computers and copies machines. A quick comparison of the theft reports and visitors' logs confirmed Mr. Castellas had been at each of the buildings prior to major thefts.

We set Herman up at a store owned by a friend of a police officer and he awaited a phone call from Castellas.

The owner of the store received a phone call from an anonymous individual who inquired about Herman's ownership of or employment with the store. Shortly thereafter, Herman received a phone call from Castellas who suggested that they meet at a coffee shop off Jefferson Boulevard on the west side. Herman was a great undercover man because he always made the criminal do the work. Herman agreed to meet Castellas and said he would want to inspect the equipment prior to purchase. Castellas became irate when Herman insisted on that condition. Herman argued that he had a store to run and was not paying for "uninspected merchandise." Castellas said that an inspection could be made if a price for the merchandise could be agreed upon.

42

On a Saturday morning at a coffee shop off Highway 41 near Jefferson Boulevard, Herman had his sitdown with Peter Castellas. On the two corners opposite from the coffee shop in two unmarked cars sat the entire Freight and Junk Squad, all of us armed with transceivers.

Herman recognized Castellas from the description he had been furnished (we also let him peek at an old mug shot) and sat down in the booth.

Castellas opened with, "You're not wired are you? 'Cause this could be a setup and I've already done my time." Herman the German immediately leaped up from his seat. "I don't have time for shit like this. I want to buy some equipment and get it to the store. Do I look like a cop? Tell me, do I look like a fuckin' cop? If that's your problem, I'm outta here. You wanna check me for a wire, go ahead!"

I looked at Boots and just shook my head.

Castellas responded, "Jesus, take it easy. You're making a scene and drawing attention to us. Sit the fuck down." Herman instantly complied and we breathed a collective sigh of relief.

Castellas did not waste any time in introducing his product line. He indicated he had about $60,000 worth of equipment that he needed to unload as his inventory was too high. Castellas said that to get rid of it he would let it go for $50,000. Herman had no money to barter with but turned that little detail around to his advantage.

"You know, I work my ass off to move used equipment and work hard for my money. I'd consider taking your problem off your hands but for $25,000 if this shit is any good." Castellas' temper started to rise and he accused Herman of trying to screw him. Herman countered with the fact that he had offered $25,000 for the equipment sight unseen and that any increase in this amount would require a physical inspection. Castellas was obviously interested in getting paid but, still unsure, suggested he would need time to think about it.

Boots turned to me and said, "Herman isn't going to give this bum time to think!"

As if Boots had been directing the conversation, Herman then said, "Look, I got the truck in the parking lot, the money close by, and not a lot of time to fuck around with you. Do I get to see it or do I walk? Your call."

I turned to Boots. "How did you know that?" Boots replied, "I've been working with that lunatic for thirty years."

Castellas caved in, the greed too much to deal with, and gave Herman an address about twenty blocks from the coffee shop where he could look at the equipment. He would meet Herman there and told him to be prepared to buy with cash in hand. The meeting was to take place in one hour.

Herman handed Castellas a check and said that now he could afford to pay for two cups of coffee.

We had already sent Special Agent Dick Herman and Detective Jim Breshnan to check out the address. It was an old storefront in the warehouse area. Its windows had been whited out. The boys observed Castellas pull up in his Cadillac and be greeted by two other men who came out of the storefront.

Boots and I met with Herman about six blocks away from the coffee shop, aware of what the other unit had observed.

Herman jumped out of the truck, pulled up his shirt, and quickly got rid of the wire and tape. Boots asked him what he was doing. "When I go in there, they'll check me for a weapon and probably a wire," Herman answered.

I looked at Boots. "He does have a point but then we have you inside blacked out of communication. Very, very risky." Herman smiled, "No go—no show. I'll use the walkie-talkie in the truck."

The clock was ticking and we agreed Herman would follow his instincts.

On our way to the location, Boots had called for two more detective units as backup and to cover of the rear of the building.

When Herman pulled up, he was all smiles. Castellas was in front with his two men. It appeared everyone was ready to do business. Herman disappeared inside the building and the most dangerous part of the operation was underway. About a half-hour had passed and Herman finally came walking out, yelling. "Gimme a minute. I gotta open the truck and get the dolly out." He hopped in the front of the cab and was on the walkie-talkie. "Boys, I think we hit pay dirt!" He then rattled off four serial numbers and equipment types. They matched our inventory list. He then said, "Kevin, I think the stickers on ninety percent of the stuff—Property of the U.S. Government—is a clue!" I responded, "Careful, lad. We aren't finished." He jumped out of the truck and returned to the building. For the next hour, t he four of them loaded the truck with a dazzling display of office equipment.

As the others re-entered the building, Herman excused himself to get a cigarette. The radio crackled. "Fellas, I told these guys I was so impressed by their inventory I'd take it all for $50,000 but only if they helped me load it on the truck. They're getting the last multicopier and I've got a little problem. I don't have $50,000 to pay them." The last copies, along with the three suspects, was making its way towards the truck.

Boots and I decided it was time to move. We drove up behind the suspects with guns drawn. Dick Herman and Jim Breshnan drove up from the other side to block any escape route.

All four, including Herman the German, were spread-eagled against the truck and taken into custody. The detectives behind the building had searched and cleared the storefront. No one else was inside.

Our Special Agent in Charge was already on the local television news with a breaking story about the end of the government office crime wave and the recovery of a quarter of a million dollars worth of stolen merchandise by the FBI in cooperation with the St. Louis Police Department.

As we watched the evening news story about our collar at a tavern near the Budweiser Brewery in South St. Louis, Herman turned to Boots. "Sergeant, how come I never get to be on T.V. and give the account of what happened?" Boots answered, "Herman, if we ever let you on T.V. the taxpayers of this city would have all of us committed!"

We all laughed, ordered another round of beer, and realized it had been a very good day.

CHAPTER FIVE

DEMOLITION MAN

Grandin,

Missouri

It was during my assignment in St. Louis, Missouri, that I became schooled in the use of explosives and how to identify and neutralize them.

I had the pleasure of working with Special Agent Dick Herman and my explosives mentor, Bill Ahler from Mississippi. Dick Herman, myself and another outstanding Special Agent, Phil Grivas, had formed a team that specialized in arresting federal fugitives and military deserters. Phil Grivas had formerly been with the New York Police Department and was an intelligent, experienced investigator who loved his work. Phil would return to New York City and become one of the elite Special Agents of that division. Since each of us had anywhere from fifty to seventy cases to work, by combining our efforts we could be even more productive. It was not unusual for us to arrest one-hundred fugitives in a month. This demanding schedule meant we worked nights, weekends and holidays to achieve the arrest figures mentioned.

After several months, I confided to the boys that I needed a break. Dick suggested I apply for an in-service school at the FBI Academy and mentioned the Bureau was looking for bombing investigation instructors. Phil commented, "Yeah, Kev, you have an explosive personality. You'll fit right in." We all laughed and I thought about it. I decided to apply for the school. We already had one instructor in the division, Bill Ahler, who was a former chemical engineer and basically a genius. Bill Ahler was a laid-back country boy and not one to get too excited about many things. He was also an analytical thinker, a keen observer of human nature, and master of the understatement. When I went to Bill to seek his advice regarding my application, he was extremely supportive and indicated he needed another Agent with whom to interact regarding bombing matters and needed help with police instructor schools in the field.

The St. Louis area at that time had been hit with a series of car bombings that had been linked to control of the plumbers union. It had gotten ugly, with several labor-related individuals having been murdered. While most of the bombings came under local jurisdiction, the police departments in the area had requested that the FBI provide more instructional schools relative to the identification of explosives and procedures to be followed to inactivate the various kinds of incendiary devices.

I packed up my bags and headed back to the FBI Academy in the beautiful Virginia countryside. The FBI Academy is located approximately fifty miles south of Washington, D.C., in the huge confines of the United States Marine Corps base at Quantico, Virginia. The Academy is the foremost law enforcement training facility in the world and trains not only police officers from the United States but, through its National Academy Program, officers from police departments all over the world.

Once I arrived at the Academy, I was assigned to a bombing instructors' in-service school with other Special Agents from all over the country, We would be trained in bomb identification and the correct procedures for handling the various difficult situations that we could expect to face. The nature and location of the mechanism, the demographic makeup of the area, and the availability of a bomb squad

51

to respond to the emergency would determine the proper procedures to be followed.

The school lasted two full weeks and was an informative session. Since the school dealt with a highly charged subject matter that could kill you, the attention span of the Agents was more intense that at other in-service schools..

Once I had completed the course, I headed back to St. Louis and linked up with Special Agent Bill Ahler to conduct police training schools. It was not long after returning that my newly found knowledge would be put to the test. A bomb threat and a bomb-sniffing dog alerted us to a suspicious suitcase located at the St. Louis International Airport and resulted in a Friday night call to the nearest "bomb expert," which was me.

I drove out to the airport and checked in with the Special Agents who covered the area. The suitcase was out on the tarmac, isolated from the passenger terminal. It was a slow news night so all of the local news media were covering the "event." If you have ever been blinded by flood lights you have an idea of what it is like facing the media. I went out to the tarmac and examined the suitcase. Since it had already been moved around we knew it contained no pressure-device or anti-disturbance mechanism which would have ignited any explosives. I decided to cut into the side of the case. There were no explosives but, instead, the entire suitcase was filled with women's lingerie. It would have served no purpose to announce the contents to the media, plus it would have made me look like a jerk. I consulted with the other Agents on the scene and we formulated a press release that read: "The FBI announced that the suitcase had been neutralized and no bomb had been found." The statement was read and no follow-up questions were entertained.

The next morning the *St. Louis Dispatch* carried a photograph of my behind on the front page, taken as I leaned over the suitcase. The caption read, "FBI Bomb Expert Examines Suspect Suitcase." My girlfriend, Pam Platts, later my wife, called me up after seeing the newspaper and said, "Nice shot. I recognized you from the rear immediately." We laughed about that picture many times over the years.

Bill and I thereafter taught several police schools and created mock crime scenes by blowing up old cars and buildings to let the officers get the feel of working a bombing crime scene. Even though we were always cautious and followed the necessary safety procedures, occasionally a car door or hood would fly over our heads. Our schools were always interesting and our students extremely attentive.

It would be a brutal bank robbery and murder in Grandin, Missouri, a small town on the edge of the Ozark Mountains, which would earn me a reputation as a bomb expert. The investigation began with a phone call to our office reporting that a banker by the name of Robert R. Kitterman, along with his wife, Bertha, and their seventeen-year-old daughter, had been kidnapped, forced to go to the bank and open the vault. The three family members could not be located.

Grandin is located at the southern tip of Missouri near the Arkansas state line. Sheriff Buford Westbrook of Carter County, Missouri, and the Missouri State Highway Patrol had responded.

Our Special Agent in Charge (SAC), William Kunkel, had been the head of the Washington (D.C.) Field Division prior to his assignment in St. Louis and had a lot of experience. He immediately recognized that this was going to be a case which would receive national attention and assembled the best investigators in the Division. Since most of these individuals, such as our bank robbery coordinator, Bob Hess, were assigned to our squad, we were given the case. Bob Hess was a professional of the highest caliber who very seldom lost his temper and gave new meaning to the phrase *cool and calm*. His partner, Jim Lummis, was a personable individual who loved a mystery and was outstanding at solving them. They would be joined by several other exceptional investigators—Special Agents Larry Cordell, Dave Cunningham, Mike Irwin and Bill Burton, the Senior Resident Agent from Popular Bluff, Missouri. Unfortunately, I did not fit into that category, according to Mr. Kunkel, so I was to man the fort in the St. Louis Office.

An information update from the Missouri State Highway Patrol indicated that three bodies, believed to be the Kittermans, had been located and that the bodies had been rigged with explosives. The officers needed a bomb expert to clear the crime scene.

Assistant Special Agent in Charge Charlie Devic called me in and said, "I guess you're going to get your wish. They need a bomb man in Grandin. Ahler's at Quantico so I guess it's you!" Charlie and I did not always see eye-to-eye but he was a good man and I respected him. The endorsement for sending me to Grandin was not overwhelming but the route there would more than make up for it.

Kevin R. Illia

The drive to Grandin from St. Louis took almost five hours, the last two on narrow mountain roads through the Ozark National Forest. The severity of the situation demanded that I get there in a hurry. I left the Federal Building in downtown St. Louis. With Special Agent Phil Grivas, an experienced driver, at the wheel, we sped at one hundred miles an h our out Highway 40 to West County Airport. A Highway Patrol plane was standing by, engines running, and I quickly belted myself into the cockpit. We immediately took off. The state trooper pilot asked if I needed any special tools and I asked for a screw driver and a pair of needle nose pliers. The pilot radioed the request and we banked left and headed south.

This was why I had joined the FBI. The car and plane ride were as exciting and dramatic as it gets, but then reality set in. I reflected on what was ahead. Dynamite? C-4? PETN? Was it booby trapped? Was there a pressure switch? What was the mechanism and could I defeat it? The questions running through my mind were endless. Shit, I could get killed. There were already three dead bodies. They say times flies when you're having fun but my thoughts were interrupted by the pilot who said, "Mr. Illia, we're setting down there!" I looked out the window – "there" was a mountain road about one hundred yards long blocked off at either end by state highway patrol cruisers.

Now I've done my share of flying and have been in a lot of planes, but this landing was going to be tight. I turned to the pilot, half kidding, and asked, "Do you do this often?" He calmly replied, "All the time, sir." The Cessna 182 then banked to the right, headed nose down over the first set of red lights on the cruiser, and landed perfectly on the dotted white line in the middle of the road. I was thrilled and expressed my sincere appreciation to the pilot. He grinned over the noise of the engine and I was out the door.

In front of me as I exited the plane was a tough looking state trooper. "You must be the demo man. These are for you." He handed me a set of needle nose pliers and a screwdriver. We watched as the plane turned around and took off. I hopped into the cruiser, red lights flashing and siren blaring, and headed up the road. After about a mile we came upon a convoy of five unmarked cars which pulled over as we passed them. I recognized the men in the cars as my fellow Special Agents who had left St. Louis four hours before.

I waved at Bob Hess as we went by and he broke into a smile and then started laughing. When we passed the lead car which contained

Special Agent in Charge Bill Kunkel, I solemnly nodded my head.

Mr. Kunkel did a double take and I could see him in the rear view

mirror mouthing the words, "Was that Illia?" I had to laugh and

thought, "Well, you can't keep a good man down."

We soon arrived at the crime scene, about five miles south of

Grandin. Carter County Sheriff Westbrook was on the scene. Sheriff

Westbrook started out, "Boy, are you the bomb man?" I replied that I

was. The Sheriff then lead me up a path past two parked cars and said,

"There they are. What are you going to do?" I said, "Study the scene

and look for explosives." The Sheriff then pointed to Mr. Kitterman's

body, which was in a sitting position and tied to a small cedar tree. He

said, "He's the only one wired." "How do you know that?" I asked.

The Sheriff answered, "Because that's what he said when he went to

the bank." I said, "I need to be absolutely sure and to do that I need to

be alone to check them out. If there's an explosive and I miscalculate

then I die with them. That's why I get paid the big bucks." The Sheriff

retorted, "Don't get smart with me, sonny. These are good town folks

and I'm in charge here!"

"Well, you can't direct an investigation if you get blown up now,

can you? I'll need some time and when it's clear you and your men can proceed." The Sheriff switched gears and simply said, "Okay, sonny. Watch yourself."

He left and the Kittermans and I were alone in the silence. As I surveyed the grisly scene, I observed that Mr. Kitterman had probably been killed first because both of the women had been tied to a nearby oak tree and there were fingernail scratches on the bark. I was furious that anyone could treat fellow human beings the way the Kittermans had been treated here. I had been on the scene of other homicides but they usually involved the murders of mobsters or gang members. This was different and I knew my fellow Agents, with all of their investigative expertise, were intent on solving this despicable act.

Then, very carefully, I walked the perimeter to insure no strings, no tripwires and no booby traps were in place. I took my time and observed everything in sight, looking for anything out of place or out of the ordinary.

Once I had done this, I approached the body of Mr. Kitterman. There was a belt around his waist, similar to a cartridge belt, but it was rigged with quarter-pound sticks of what appeared to be dynamite. Wires ran from the back on each side of the belt. I thought to myself, "No mistakes, Big Kev, or they'll be doing a crime scene for four." I carefully lifted a portion of Mr. Kitterman's jacket and followed the wires to the back of the belt.

I was perspiring and nervous as I lifted up the rest of the jacket. The wires ran back into two of the quarter-pound sticks. No remote control device and no apparent triggering device were visible. I gingerly pushed one of the receiving sticks out of its holder. It was the same size as the rest and had no other fuses in it. As I turned it over, I could read a partial word – "HIGHW…" "Son-of-a-bitch!," I thought, "These are highway flares!"

Before I got too excited I examined the other sticks and the wires. Nothing! I decided to cut the wire, realizing that a collapsing circuit could still cause a detonation. The device was not sophisticated, however, and the circuit idea was probably beyond the ability of the builder. Snip. Snip. No explosion occurred. I examined the rest of the sticks – definitely highway flares.

I went over to the bodies of the two women. They had not been sexually molested and an examination of each disclosed no improvised explosive devices attached to them. I stood and gazed at the scene before me, said a quick prayer for the Kittermans, and then walked down the dirt road.

The SAC and the other Special Agents had arrived and were being briefed by Sheriff Westbrook. As I came closer the SAC looked inquiringly at me. I said, "The scene is clear. There were highway flares on Mr. Kitterman rigged to appear to be an explosive device. No other explosive devices located." The SAC glanced quickly at the other Agents and said, "Let's go."

Once the investigation got underway, the cooperation between the various law enforcement agencies involved was outstanding. All of the officers were as outraged as I was at this senseless act of violence.

Special Agent Bill Burton, whose territory covered Grandin, would do an exceptional job of following up on the investigation, prosecution and, ultimately, the conviction in Jefferson County Circuit Court, Hillsboro, Missouri, of the individuals who committed the murders. The three men, Dallas R. Delay, Jerry Rector and Lloyd Cowin, were each sentenced to life imprisonment by Circuit Court Judge Phillip G. Hess.

The "Demo Man" had established a reputation and would move on to other cases.

The author (middle) with U.S. Navy Seals at their base in the Caribbean.

Agent Man on undercover assignment loading scuba gear for "Snowflake" in St. Croix harbor, U.S. Virgin Islands.

The author greeting then Governor of Puerto Rico the
Hon. Carlos Romero Barcelo at Military hanger near San Juan.

In a rare photo (Lt. to Rt.), the author, "Jerry the Forger", and contact
agent Robert E. Spiel.

The author disembarking from Huey Helicopter after aerial security survey of Puerto Rico

Agent Man "on repel" from helicopter during anti-terrorist training.

(Lt. to Rt.) Special Agents Marie "The Profiler" Dyson, Jack "Monsignor" O'Rourke, the author, Bob "Polish Prince" Scigalski, and Dave "Stealth" Steele in undercover van before narcotics raid.

Surveillance photo near Isla de Culebra where smuggling ship "Esmeralda" was moored.

Agent Man on special operations boat at a U.S. Naval Base in the Caribbean.

CHAPTER SIX

SAILING ON THE SNOWFLAKE

St. Croix

United States Virgin Islands

The wheels lifted off the ground as the American Airlines island hopper headed for St. Croix in the United States Virgin Islands.

As I gazed out the window at the dark blue Atlantic Ocean, the palm trees waving in the breeze and the white sand, a buffer between the sea and the swaying trees, I was reminded what a beautiful island Puerto Rico is, resting just south of the United States mainland.

The plane had about twenty passengers aboard and you could read them like books. The Puerto Rican businessmen in their traditional guyabara shirts with accompanying leather briefcases. They were the "day-trippers" commuting to the Virgin Islands for a day of business meetings and then back to San Juan and a short drive to their "casas." The "mainlanders," young couples all in white on their honeymoons, were totally engrossed in each other to the exclusion of everyone else, filled with the excitement of an "exotic" island on their first trip away from mom and dad. This time the sex would be legal and the anticipation showed on their faces. I envied them, but now it was time to concentrate on the business at hand.

I had been in the Caribbean for about a year, assigned to the FBI Field Office in San Juan. The island of Puerto Rico is bordered on its northern coast by the Atlantic Ocean and on its southern coast by the calm Caribbean Sea. The tropical heat, the exotic surroundings, and the dominance of the beautiful but foreign Spanish language when mixed with the violence of terrorism made this field office not the most popular or sought-after in the FBI and occasionally contributed to bizarre behavior on the part of some of our Special Agents.

I arrived there in January, 1977. During my first week in the office a supervisor tried to strangle the Special Agent in Charge (SAC) because he wanted off the island. The supervisor *did* have a drinking problem and needed medical help, which he received. Seeing the supervisor climbing over the SAC's desk in order to get a piece of him and the SAC yelling, "Take him to Rosie Roads for evaluation," was not reassuring to me. The U.S. Naval Hospital was located on the east end of the island at Roosevelt Roads Naval Base and it was a good thing the hospital was there.

As the plane lumbered up the north coast of Puerto Rico we passed over the beautiful beach at Luquillo and then made a slight course correction east. The view now was of the clouds in the distance over the humid and lush rain forest of El Yunque. Several hundred inches of rain fall each year over the mountain range of El Yunque, usually in the late afternoon. The fauna and flora of the area make it a must stop for anyone visiting the interior of Puerto Rico.

As we continued east we started to go "down island," toward the Caribbean Sea which has always been a calmer, more tranquil body of water than the pounding Atlantic.

I had been assigned to an anti-terrorist squad which worked terrorist cells on the island. The terrorists plain and simple wanted independence for Puerto Rico. The whole history of the Island—its relationship with Spain after that country invaded Puerto Rico, the United States' invasion during the Spanish-American War, and the displacement of the Spanish government—led to the independence movement becoming a focal point for a small minority of Puerto Ricans. There are no independent islands that can exist without some type of assistance from a world power. The Puerto Rican terrorist movement h as always been a pro-Marxist-Leninist ideology but in today's world cannot expect serious assistance from either Cuba or Russia. It is important to differentiate between the *violent* terrorist movement and the Puerto Rican Independence Movement (PIP), which is a legitimate political party headed by some of the most brilliant minds on the island.

My neighbors were "independentistas" and many an hour did we sit around with a few Coronas in hand discussing the movement. My neighbors were both highly educated and extremely intelligent but had a political vision of Puerto Rico as an independent country with no ties to the United States. While our political beliefs were divergent we became close friends and I was treated to an insider's view of Puerto Rican culture and politics few "gringos" ever were able to enjoy because my neighbors realized I had a deep interest in Puerto Rican culture and customs and sincerely wanted to learn about the island and its people.

The drone of the aircraft was loud and actually helped me to concentrate on what I needed to do. Certain arrangements had been made in advance and due to the fact that some of the sources may still be operational I will dispense with the specifics and move on to the mission.

In the lovely little town of Christiansted, with its Danish architecture, picturesque harbor, and lovely little shops, can be found the Comanche Bar and Hotel. I was to contact a grizzly old operative who had been in the islands for years and was rumored to have slipped out of Berlin in the waning days of 1945 with some help from U.S. intelligence.

Gertie was not one of those people you instantly warm up to and want to share a tent with during a torrential downpour. I had observed him briefly with our contact Agent, Doug Jones, and realized this guy could care less what you had to say as long as it came with the cash compensation.

On this particular day the plane landed at Alexander Hamilton Airport, now Rholson Airport, and I proceeded directly to an open-air taxi. A regular taxi is more expensive because of the air conditioning. Passing through the sloping hills and beautiful vegetation of St. Croix, I am reminded that while the islands appear to be paradise, as the real estate brokers would lead you to believe, they actually have many of the same problems found everywhere—a high unemployment rate, an unskilled labor force, a struggling educational system and drug use by the youthful population. Because of the long periods of drought in the islands, a threat to the livelihood of the islanders, the issue of an adequate supply of fresh drinking water is a constant concern.

We soon weave our way on the narrow roads into the lovely harbor town of Christiansted. The United States acquired the Virgin Islands in 1913 from Denmark. The town's Danish-influenced architecture makes it one of the most beautiful and unique sights in these islands. The Cruzans, as the people like to be called, are warm and friendly, take pride in their heritage, and have a deep faith that is demonstrated in the churches across the island every Sunday morning. Life on St. Croix is not easy and making a living in the service industry, wherein the majority of the population works, means long hours and inadequate pay.

There is also what a lot of tourists call the "race issue." There is a huge disparity between the white tourists who work hard all year to be able to vacation here and the people of St. Croix, predominantly black, who observe only white "rich" folks coming to their island and demanding service. The tourists often do not understand the history and culture of the islanders, including the Cruzans. The natives of St.

Croix, like those on most of the islands of the Caribbean, operate at a slower pace, which is a part of the island's charm. The tourists from New York, Los Angeles, Chicago or Denver are not "geared down" when they hit the island. Hence, a conflict can occur and usually does.

As I get out of the taxi I am reminded that the heat of the islands is different than that of Puerto Rico. It hangs in the air and no breeze blows in the stillness of the harbor. It is good to be back and I head down Strand Street all the way to Comanche Walk. On the corner is the famous Comanche Hotel. As I enter the bar, a few familiar faces can be seen. I am dressed in my usual white Panama hat, khaki safari shorts, sneakers with a white guyabera shirt and a red bandana around my neck. I peer across the well-used wooden bar and sight Gertie on his usual stool at the end of the bar, sipping a beer. Gertis is in his early sixties, white beard, balding, wearing a tan safari shirt and matching pants. He wears a small pair of black framed glasses low on his nose. He looks like a professor in Germanic studies but alertly picks up on my entrance.

I walk to the end of the bar and reintroduce myself, "Hi, I'm Superman. I met you at Doug Jones' a few months back." Gertie sizes me up and says, "I've been expecting you. Do you want a beer?" I

74

respond, "No thanks, but maybe a Coca Cola." The bartender has been most observant and the Coke immediately appears on the wooden counter. Gertie starts to laugh. "You FBI types are all alike. Goody-goody." I smile and think to myself, "Well, we were good enough to kick your ass during World War II," but decide that is not a good way to start off the conversation. Instead I decide to stick to business. "I understand you have a boat and a good skipper for me?"

Gertie answers, "Here, this is gonna be tough. You walk out the door, down the street, make a left on King's Alley. Look for a sloop with the name 'Snowflake.' Got it?"

"Yeah, I think I can remember that! What's the skipper's name?" Gertie replies, "Solomon. He's a little screwy but he knows every harbor in the British Virgin Islands."

I decide it's time to go over the whole program with Gertie so that I make no mistakes. I say, "So, let me get this straight. I'm looking for a sloop named Snowflake and a guy named Skipper Solomon. Is that correct?" Gertie tersely answers, "Yeah."

"Okay," I reply. It's time to leave but before I do I buy Gertie a shot of Bushmill's whiskey which he promptly puts away. It has been a passable visit but I still have misgivings about Gertie. He is one of those personalities who if the Nazis had won would have been comfortable working for them. I learned a long time ago that as I journied through my FBI career I would meet a lot of people who do a lot of different things for a lot of different reasons. It always struck me that if you did what you were supposed to do, worked within the law, and remembered which side you were on, things would probably work out.

As I walked out of the Comanche the bright glare of the sun struck my eyes. I waited a few moments until my eyes adjusted, then headed toward the docks. As I strode down King's alley, I noticed an outdoor café with blue umbrellas and checked red and white table cloths framed by palm trees overhead. I recalled that while at one time the café was known as Café de Paris and had served the best lobster salad in the Caribbean, it was now under new management and under another name.

I kept on walking and soon came into view of the sparkling turquoise water of the Caribbean in the Christiansted harbor. I stepped on to the wooden dock and began to search for the Snowflake. There was a motor boat in the water with a white hull and white finish that looked brand new. Next to it was a thirty foot, two-mast with a blue hull and the name "El Gato," the cat.

I continued to search for the ship in the bright sunlight. As I neared the end of the dock, I spotted a single-masted boat with a green hull and a faded brown teak deck bearing the name Snowflake. It was a sloop, approximately thirty-five feet long, in need of a great deal of repair. But then again, I was on my government budget and could not expect to see the "Sea Goddess" taking me on as a passenger.

As I approached the Snowflake, I observed a tall black Cruzan man in a white shirt and purple shorts on deck who immediately spotted me. He walked up to me with a smile on his face and shouted, "I'm Solomon and you must be the Agent Man." I returned his smile, turned, looked around and then replied, "Yeah, that's right, Solomon. A little bit louder just in case there's a terrorist in the Caribbean that hasn't heard you and doesn't get a shot at me!" He laughed heartily and I knew we would get along just fine on our new adventure as long as he kept his mouth shut.

I would find out very soon that while Solomon was spontaneous and loved to talk, he also knew his business and would become my most important resource over the next five days.

The weather was beautiful and as the wind caught the sail we picked up the speed that would propel the Snowflake through the water as if it were gliding across an ice floe. We were free from the cares of the world and as the island of St. Croix grew smaller behind us, I realized that I really enjoyed sailing. There is a peace and tranquility on the ocean that is not duplicated anywhere else on earth. I think scuba diving has this same appeal. Man is one with the sea and becomes part of the landscape of the reef, another creature caught in the natural splendor of the ocean with nothing to distract from the enjoyment of the awesome beauty below the surface of the water. It is a singular experience.

Solomon had observed my quiet reflection and gave me space to enjoy the salt air, the deep blue of the Caribbean, and the silent power of the wind propelling us through the water. We headed north through Pillsbury Sound and then east through "The Narrows."

After about three hours and having passed Joust van Dyke Island, Solomon spoke up. "So, Agent Man, what are we after?" I answered,

"Solomon, the name is Kevin, an old island name from the Emerald Isle, many miles from here."

"Well, I could have you call me 'Captain,' and I know where Ireland is located!" Solomon replied sharply. "I'll leave the other title behind, Kevin. I just would like to know what we are doing out here."

"All right, Solomon, I'll lay it out for you. We're looking for a forty to forty-five foot ship called the 'Esmeralda.' She set sail from St. Georges, Grenada, about three days ago headed, we believe, for Puerto Rico. The information I have is she has explosives, rocket launchers and small arms on board for delivery to the Machateros terrorist group led by Filiberto Ojeda-Rios. The delivery of those supplies won't enhance the domestic tranquility of the enchanted island of Puerto Rico."

Solomon stared at me in stunned silence for a few seconds and then smiled. "This is groovy, man! I always wanted to be a secret agent on the right side."

"What are you talking about, Solomon?" I asked. "This is serious shit. These guys aren't some Jamaican steel band on a gig. This is terrorist shit and people get killed." Solomon smiled. "That's why I love you, Kevin. You are Agent Man! Now, how about some great

79

Cruzan rum?" Solomon then produced a bottle of white rum and proceeded to consume half of it as though it were a bottle of Evian. I laughed and hoped he could sail the Snowflake as well as he handled the fifth of rum.

The plan called for us to sail into the ports down island, specifically Tortola, Beef Island and Virgin Gorda in the British Virgin Islands, in an attempt to locate the ship. U.S. intelligence had estimated that the travel time from Grenada, as well as the exposure time at sea, would cause the Esmeralda to put into port in order to resupply and also to blend in with other pleasure craft that heavily used this route. I fully concurred with this hypothesis. The worst case scenario would be that we locate the ship and have a dangerous encounter with the crew. Looking back at Solomon emptying a second bottle of rum, I thought that *would* be the worst case scenario. The *best* would be that we search for the boat, do not find it, and enjoy five beautiful days at sea, compliments of the U.S. Government. While that appealed to my romantic side, it would only delay big problems later on in Puerto Rico. No, we needed to do our best to locate that ship before it reached the beaches of Puerto Rico.

Finally, I turned to Solomon, who by this time was in a total state of "relaxation" at the helm of his ship. "Solomon, we need to find this Esmeralda, not to engage her but to identify her position and transmit it back to a team I have standing by."

Solomon smiled and said, "My friend, that is a relief. I had reservations as to how even two talented men such as ourselves could pull this off.!"

We sailed toward Virgin Gorda, our first stop, and a well-used port for yachts sailing up and down the Sir Francis Drake passage. As we sailed into the harbor of Spanish Town I realized what an enormous task this was going to be. There were a daunting number of vessels moored in the harbor, not to mention those anchored away from the docks. It was a beautiful sight, so tranquil and peaceful; hard to imagine that anyone sailing these lovely waters would carry with them the tools of death and destruction.

I turned to Solomon who, I sensed, had already read my thoughts. "We have to find these assholes and neutralize them," I said. "This is too beautiful a scene to have people like this destroy it."

"I know, man," replied Solomon, "I have a family that I am raising in these islands."

We docked at a mooring and I headed to see the harbormaster about docking fees and port information. While there, on a pretext of looking for some friends, I was able to review the list of the boats in the harbor, none of which was the object of our interest. Meanwhile, Solomon was cleaning the Snowflake and stowing the sails.

We headed to dinner at the Crag Hole, which, despite its name, was a nice dining spot overlooking the beautiful harbor and within walking distance of the docks.

After drinks, and before our fish dinner arrived, we discussed how to divide up our duties and search routines. Solomon had traveled throughout these islands and had many friends who kept abreast of the boats' comings and goings for a variety of reasons. I didn't want to know the reasons but I *did* want to reap the benefit of their observations. Solomon said he understood and would handle that aspect. I would assume my usual dumb-ass tourist role, which meant asking a lot of questions and peeking at a few more hotel registers and h arbor lists. Surveying the boats in the harbors would be a combined effort. We had a plan and we were executing it!

The next morning we sailed out of Spanish Town. After surveying the boats in the harbor, we decided to head past "The Baths," which is a beach near Stoney Bay with natural rock formations that look as though huge boulders had been rolled into the sea. It is a beautiful location and can be explored both on land and in the water. We decided to circumnavigate the island to insure we had not missed anything, heading past Copper Mine Bay, around Sound Bluff, and on to Pargaros Point.

Our next port of call was Beef Island, the smallest of the British West Indies, and also the site of an airport and landing strip. We checked out the harbor, such as it was, at Bluff Bay but to no avail. We decided to tie up for lunch.

Rodney Smallcross, the proprietor of Rodney's Reggae Restaurant, was a friend of Solomon's and greeted us with open arms. Rodney also stocked "Red Stripe," my favorite Jamaican beer.

After lunch we headed back toward the Snowflake. Solomon confided in me that Rodney had been in the "business" and knew the routes. I didn't even want to ask. "I take it we aren't talking about the restaurant industry.?"

"Kevin, we have to head around Tortola. The ship, the Esmeralda, is there near Shark Bay!" Solomon exclaimed excitedly.

As I hoisted the jib sail, I was amazed at how fast Solomon could move on board his boat. He was a fine sailor and we left Beef Island for the north side of Tortola.

Dusk had fallen as we passed Shark Bay and entered Brewer's Bay. There row after row of yachts stood like sentinels against an orange Caribbean sunset that enveloped the skies over these lovely islands. When I joined the FBI, I had never imagined that I would one day watch a beautiful sunset in the Caribbean and actually get paid for it.

We surveyed the harbor and then tied up. I checked in with the harbormaster and asked if he had heard of the ship Esmeralda. He reviewed his records and indicated it had been in port that afternoon for refueling and had left. There was a crew of five aboard and they were not a pleasant lot.

When I returned to our mooring, Solomon already knew the story. We decided to leave at first light of dawn so that we would not pass them in the night. We had dinner and Solomon went back to the boat while I made some phone calls to San Juan.

"Kevin, where are you?" asked Lt. Commander Nick "Goldie" Goldstein of the U.S. Navy. Nick was a tough Jewish kid from New

Jersey who commanded Caribbean Detachment #2 of the U.S. Navy SEAL Team stationed at the naval Base in Puerto Rico.

"Nick, we just missed them. They were here a few hours ago and left!" I said. "We're going to pursue them at first light." Nick listened and then responded, "I have a ten man SEAL team ready to launch but I'd like to send up a jet if you can give us a location."

"We'll hopefully have that for you tomorrow. By the way, there are five aboard," I told him. Nick grunted, "Okay, just find that ship for us."

"Well, I can guarantee you it's not headed for Cuba, Nick." I was restless and decided that a beer was in order.

I finished the beer and headed toward the waterfront. Just as I reached the dock area, two men walked by and one asked the time. I looked down at my watch. It was 10:30 P.M. As I looked up I saw that the second man was holding a knife. He said, "We'd like your wallet, also."

I thought for a moment: I'm in the middle of a terrorist investigation and these two buffoons are out on a robbery spree. Somehow they had managed to pick on the only white tourist on the entire island of Tortola who was carrying a fifteen-shot 9 mm Sig

Sauer. This situation presented a dilemma. If I wasted these two, I would blow my cover and lose the opportunity to pursue the much more important goal of pursuing an arms boat. But, since I work hard for a living, these bastards were out of luck.

Before I could reach for my automatic, from out of the darkness came the distinctive crack of a shotgun and a voice threatening, "My brothers, you have two choices. To die where you stand or to run like hell!" They were gone, and out of the shadows, grinning ear to ear, Solomon emerged.

"You're full of surprises, my man," I said. He laughed and we retired for the evening.

Before dawn we quietly glided out of Tortola and after clearing the harbor were under full sail. I had brought a pair of heavy lenses to scan the horizon. We both knew what was at stake and Solomon set a direct course toward Puerto Rico. We sailed down the West End past Great Thatch Island and on to St. Thomas.

As the crisp early morning air turned into the pleasant warmth of the morning breeze, we passed three boats, two heading down island and one in our direction. As we sailed past the islands of Great St. James and Little St. James, I realized we were on the south side of St.

Thomas and we had to pass only Culebra and Vieques Islands before we reached Puerto Rico.

I scanned the seashore for the silhouette of the Esmeralda. "Nothing, Solomon," I said. "Could they have altered course and decided to take another route?" Solomon looked at me anxiously but replied, "No, Kevin. They're here and they're on this route. Rodney no lie."

I thought to myself, "Oh yeah. I'm pinning a whole terrorist investigation on a reggae singer named 'Red Stripe' Rodney who used to be a smuggler. I better start drinking some of that Cruzan rum because the sun has definitely fried my brain."

As I sat forward near the jib sail I was in a reflective mood. Where or what should be our next move? Solomon, from behind the helm, interrupted my thoughts. "There, in the inlet, anchored!" I grabbed my binoculars. The description matched but I could not see the name. We were near Culebra Island. "Solomon, we need to get on the port side so I can identify her." We began to maneuver to the starboard and as we did, the rear of the anchored ship came into view.

"Son of a bitch. The reggae guy was right, Solomon. It *is* the Esmeralda!"

There was no activity on the deck which meant the crew was either on the island or asleep. We needed to get hold of "Goldie" and his bears, or, in this case, his SEALS. Solomon wasted no time in tacking and heading toward the small town of Dewey on the west side of Culebra Island.

We pulled up to the dock. I found a public phone and made the call. Nick answered the phone. I said, "It's me and they're anchored at Soni on Culebra." Nick responded, "We'll handle it from here. Nice job!"

I returned to the Snowflake, extremely relieved. Solomon was still tense, and asked, "Where to, Kevin?" "I think home to Christiansted, Solomon. Our assignment's finished. Besides, you haven't had a rum with ice in almost a week." Solomon laughed as we shoved off for St. Croix.

We arrived back in St. Croix a few hours later, secured the Snowflake, and decided to meet for breakfast. Solomon had been away from his family and was anxious to see them. I dined at the Commanche and then stayed the night.

The next morning we met at a dockside café. Solomon had a newspaper he had picked up on his way to our meeting. On the third page of the paper was a small article concerning a ship that had sunk and five illegal Grenadans who had been detained by the U.S. Coast Guard. The accident had been attributed to an explosion in the engine room. The ship was identified as the Esmeralda, registered in St. Georges, Grenada.

After breakfast I paid Solomon for his services and added a sizable bonus. I was trying to figure out how I would voucher it but he had definitely earned it.

Solomon drove me to the airport and we said goodbye. "Kevin, if you ever need another boat for hire, I'm here!" Solomon said. "Thanks, Solomon. I know and I will not forget."

CHAPTER SEVEN

WILLIE THE WIRETAPPER

Chicago,

Illinois

Wallace William Wagoner was born in Chicago in 1935 and by 1950 had been arrested three times, twice for auto theft and once for burglary.

Wally was a jovial type of criminal who made more than his share of mistakes in his life and was known on a first-name basis by a series of wardens at the Illinois State Penitentiary near Joliet.

Wally had the distinction of having a seven-page rap-sheet and had served three four-year terms at the correctional facility for a total of twelve years in jail. The simple fact was that Wally had become a career criminal and needed to either reform his life or change his "modus operandi" since, so far, it had been a total failure.

Wally decided to do the latter and some time after his last release, and when he came to the attention of the FBI, he became "Willie the Wiretapper."

It later became known, as we reconstructed "Willie the Wiretapper" Wagoner's life, that during his prison incarceration he took up the study of electronics. The prison staff was elated, believing that finally Wagoner was getting his act together, would join a labor union in Chicago, and become a productive member of society.

As Willie saw it, excuse the pun, the lights went on and he could finally make some money as a "wire man" for some street burglary crews in Chicago. He became so proficient at it and gained such a reputation that he acquired not only his nickname but also an invitation from the Chicago mob to debug some of their hangouts and insure the FBI was not listening in on their conversations. Luckily for us, the mobsters had a penchant for talking about hiring "Willie the Wiretapper" to check the place out before he had actually done the work!

This gave us time to either shut down our operation or cause it to go "silent" while Willie went about his work. He never found an FBI bug so we were happy. The mobsters were happy because their hangout was not compromised and Willie was happy because he collected a hefty fee for his technical ability.

Willie developed such a reputation in the Chicago underworld that he began to instruct aspiring young burglars on how to circumvent alarm systems developed by major security systems manufacturers. As an enterprising criminal, Willie had few peers.

It was during this period of economic prosperity that the seeds of Willie's next downfall were sown. He was now in his late forties and had always enjoyed the company of ladies. He was also known to imbibe a few cocktails along the way. Willie had never married because he had really not had the time to develop any long-time relationships due to his intermittent "vacations" in Joliet. As the extroverted individual he was, after a few drinks he would regale the ladies with stories about his criminal exploits and how he had outsmarted the law. He would usually throw in the part about his being an ex-con but without elaborating that he was a three-time loser.

Willie became a well known figure on the North Side of Chicago in the pubs and taverns near Wrigley Field. It appeared that Willie made the rounds in the neighborhood buying drinks for everyone, flirting with the ladies, and always having plenty of money. During the daytime, Willie slept off his overindulgence.

It was during this period that he came up with his retirement plan. He had researched several banks in the Chicago and Indiana area and, because of a number of factors, decided that he could pull off one more big job by knocking off a bank, thereby insuring his retirement and a continuation of his lifestyle.

While not rich, Willie had made enough money so that he was living in a high-rise apartment on Addison Street with a lovely view of Lake Michigan from his balcony. He now had a live-in girlfriend twenty years his junior and it appeared his income may have enhanced his sex appeal as his features would not have put him on the cover of *Gentleman's Quarterly*.

It was about this time that I was introduced to the ongoing adventures of Willie the Wiretapper. The FBI has a network of various sources of information which is the life blood of any successful investigative agency. It is these sources that provide the information to enable a law enforcement agency to focus its time and resources where they need to be to solve a crime or, in this case, to prevent it from happening. Two of these sources indicated that Willie had picked out a bank in Indiana, had checked out its alarm system in order to neutralize it, and, knowing the schedule of currency deliveries, had chosen a day and time to hold up the bank for optimum return.

Since this information came from two independent sources, we decided that Willie Wagoner would garner closer attention from Special Agents of the FBI.

At the time I was working on Squad C-2, a criminal squad in the Chicago Office, headed by a hard-charging former Marine, Joe Brennan, with a cast of Special Agents as colorful as Willie and two hundred times smarter. Joe Brennan did not want Willie pulling a bank robbery we knew about prior to the event and then possibly hurting any citizens during the commission of a federal felony. He decided, given Willie's track record, and, with the agreement of the entire squad, that we would concentrate our efforts on Willie.

The squad was made up of seasoned investigators, such as Peter J. Wacks, who, after retirement, would serve as one of the congressional investigators in the Clinton impeachment hearings, and John "Father" O'Rourke, who gained that name through his unique ability to get even the most notorious criminals to confess after a session with

"Himself". Also on the squad was Bob "The Polish Prince" Scigalski who, as a hostage negotiator, caused many a hostage-taker to surrender because no one could ever talk longer than "The Prince".

The team of Bob "The Italian Stallion" Pecoraro and Wayne "The Gun" Zydron were kind of the Siegfried and Roy of the squad, always working together, always entertaining, and always very successful.

Also on Squad C-2 was John "Johnny D" Dolan, a brilliant investigator who specialized in multimillion dollar frauds or swindles at the Chicago financial exchanges. John was the type of agent who inspired confidence and reflected the best of the FBI. He would work up a case on his own and, at the critical arrest period would involve the entire squad, which made us all look good.

Special Agent Jeff "The Gent" Boggan was a southern gentleman close to retirement but always ready to "hit the street" and share his enormous knowledge with his fellow agents.

The idea of placing a full-blown surveillance on Willie the Wiretapper created some unique problems. We had developed information that his live-in girlfriend had some contacts in the FBI which meant that the operation must only be known to members of Squad C-2.

It also occurred to us that given Willie's interest in electronics and security, he would probably have a scanner system directed at the Chicago Police Department and possibly the FBI. This assumption proved correct later on as it turned out that Willie had a scanner for at least four other major police agencies in the area and made it a point to locate the frequency of those Indiana police agencies in the area of the bank.

In order to defeat his elaborate security, our FBI technicians came up with a scrambler communication system which would allow us to communicate during a surveillance but would defeat Willie's efforts to locate our frequencies. The beauty of it was that it also precluded the Chicago news media, an outstanding group of investigators in their own right, from intercepting or compromising our operations.

There was also the small problem of Willie's being a career criminal who knew how to "dry clean" himself and who was very alert to police surveillance. This was overcome with some surveillance techniques still in use and which will not be elaborated upon in deference to the Special Agents who carry on this most important work while protecting the American public.

Once we were up and running, the entire squad was committed and dedicated to finding out if Willie was really a bank robber in addition to being a wiretapper.

Willie's pattern of staying up late at the taverns and sleeping late in the mornings caused us to adjust our approach to our duties and schedules.

On one of the first evenings of "Operation Willie Won't He" we had a problem. Bob Pecoraro and Jeff Boggan entered a pub to observe Willie. Willie immediately made them as cops and announced it to the entire bar. Jeff answered that they were only working guys trying to enjoy the evening. The two agents sat there and drank away. We were sitting in cars one block away when Bob came out of the tavern three hours later. He headed to Wayne's vehicle in an unsteady manner. Wayne radioed that Bob was all right but smelled like a brewery.

About an hour later, Jeff came stumbling out, made his way to the car I was in, and passed out in the back seat.

"Father" O'Rourke came to the rescue. He entered the tavern and quickly took up Jeff's barstool, which was still warm. An hour later out walked Willie, totally in control of his faculties, and headed home. "Father" O'Rourke indicated the subject of our surveillance had an enormous ability to consume the hops and grain alcohol. He suggested, given our two casualties, that we needed to reconsider our approach.

It was decided the next day at a squad conference that there would be an hourly rotation in the pubs as Willie had already proved he could outlast any of our agents in the bar. "The Polish Prince" indicated he and "Father" O'Rourke had received information that Willie had arranged for the purchase of weapons from a particular individual with a criminal record. The purchase was to be made that afternoon in an alley off Clark Street.

We immediately sent units to the North Side to discreetly survey the alley and to arrange a surveillance.

About three in the afternoon a black Lincoln Continental was driven slowly down the alley. The driver paid no attention to the Commonwealth Edison truck parked in the alley near a utility pole. A few minutes later, Willie appeared driving a green Jeep Cherokee. The exchange took less than five minutes as the trunk on the Continental popped open and the mobile gun shop was in business.

Willie was not a shy customer. He checked the action on two pump shotguns and the slides on two fifteen-shot automatics, paid cash—no credit cards on this transaction—and then left. The mystery man in the Continental turned out to be "Blacky" Tarton, a fringe criminal who supplied anything and everything to the Chicago mob.

The time spent in the alley in the Commonwealth Edison truck was productive because we had our first violation, a convicted criminal in possession of illegal firearms. It was a blessing, but a curse too, in that we now had Willie armed with something other than a set of pliers.

The next day Willie was out the door by 9:00 A.M., totally out of character for him. The green Jeep rolled down Addison Street, south on Lake Shore Drive to Oak Street, where he stopped and picked up his girlfriend. The girlfriend got behind the wheel as Willie moved to the passenger side. We were all excited since this type of activity seemed to indicate that there was some kind of agenda being played out.

The Jeep was driven around the North Side and then headed west on Ontario Street. After about an hour we were still not sure if he was dry-cleaning himself. The Jeep suddenly stopped in the middle of the street. Willie walked up to a white Chevy van, spent a few minutes near the door, entered the vehicle and pulled away. One of our units made a check on the van's license plate and learned its owner was listed as a Diego Garcia.

It appeared we had our second violation—auto theft. Willie was then followed to Earl Schieb's Auto Paint Palace. Earl's claim to fame was that for $59.99 you could get your entire car painted. Of course, that was the advertised price and for an additional hundred dollars the car would be waxed, baked and made to look like new. Willie, being nervous and in a hurry, went with the $59.99 special. In what may have been the fastest paint job in Earl Schieb's history, Willie was out of there in forty-five minutes! The midnight blue actually looked better than the original color, except for the wet paint dripping from the frame looked very strange. When one of the agents asked which way Willie had turned, the car radio crackled with the reply, "Just follow the ink spots on the road."

The telephone tapes that night indicated Willie needed two accomplices. The two were recruited, luckily one was a criminal informant working for the FBI. Willie met them at a pub three blocks from Wrigley Field and laid out the job. Willie and our man would enter the bank after Willie h ad neutralized the alarm system. The third man would drive the Earl Schieb special. The split would be sixty percent for Willie and twenty percent for each of the others.

The job was set to go the next day to insure that no security was breached and to get it done quickly.

Our plan was to wire our informant, follow the van until it crossed the state line, and then take it down.

Early the next morning we met in the squad room long before other employees began arriving. We checked out our bulletproof vests, shotguns, sidearms, ammo supply and raid jackets. Since I was qualified to handle an H & K MP-5 submachine gun, I checked one out of the vault with four twenty-round magazines.

Willie and his accomplices met at his apartment and then headed toward Indiana. The night before, he and his girlfriend had parked the green Jeep about two miles from the bank and then drove back to Chicago. It would be the "switch car" that would replace the van after the robbery.

As the van moved out, the parade began. In front of the van, paralleling it, and in back of the van were FBI cars. The van stopped en route at a Dunkin Donuts shop. Not sure whether Willie had paid for his donuts or not, we waited nervously for the operation to continue.

Shortly after the van crossed the state line, it pulled off Interstate 65 at Merrillville, Indiana, for gas. We observed one of the men gassing the van while the other two entered the gas station, coming out with snacks in their hands.

The radio crackled, "Take 'em down!" In an instant the Shell Station looked like a movie set. Pete Wacks and I closed in from behind, my finger throwing the selector switch of my H & K to full automatic. Pete pulled out his Sig Sauer as we drove into the station. "Father" O'Rourke and "The Polish Prince" approached from the side, with Bob Pecoraro and Wayne Zydron blocking the front.

Willie looked bewildered and dropped his Twinkies and his Big Gulp drink.

In the subsequent search of the van, we found the scanners were on, and there were ski masks and weapons in the back, along with a diagram of the bank.

Willie would do five years in a federal prison before he would return to Chicago.

On the day of his release I was walking in downtown Chicago near the Loop, when a voice yelled out, "Hey, Superman! I'm back!" It was "Willie the Wiretapper" Wagoner, and, yes h e was back.

CHAPTER EIGHT

JERRY THE FORGER

Chicago,

Illinois

While working the Night Supervisor position at the Chicago Field Office of the FBI, I received a distressing call from a man who wished to speak with Speical Agent Robert Spiel. Bob was on my squad, a reserved man who had graduated from Yale University and specialized in art theft cases. With his amazing abilities Bob had recovered several major stolen art pieces in and around the Chicago area over the past several years.

The voice at the other end of the phone blurted out, "This is Jerry. I got some big fuckin' problems and I need to talk to Bob Spiel now." Since it was one o'clock on a Sunday morning I was reluctant to call Bob unless it was a dire emergency so I said, "Jerry, this has got to be important. In case you haven't noticed, it's one a.m. on Sunday."

"Listen, lughead, I got a dead body in bed of some young guy who overdosed and a dumpster under my apartment window," Jerry responded. "You figure it out!"

"I don't know what the hell you're talking about. Let's start from the beginning," I said.

This was my introduction to Jerry "The Forger" Dillion. Jerry was a career criminal who had all the vices and none of the virtues but did have a God-given talent for painting.

Meanwhile, back on the phone, I inquired how he had arrived at his present situation and what he intended to do about it. Jerry explained it this way: "I meet this good looking young man at a bar. We have a few drinks then go back to my place. He wants more beer before we get it on. I run to the store, get a six-pack, return to find him overdosed in my bed and no pulse. Well, being a convicted felon, this is no good for me. So, I walk around the apartment, look out the window, see the dumpster down below, and remember they pick up at five a.m. I'll just slide him out the window. Problem solved."

Right there I interjected. "Wow, Jerry. You can't just dump a dead body in a dumpster after telling an FBI Agent what happened." It's now one-thirty in the morning and I couldn't believe this surreal conversation was actually taking place. I also realized Jerry was right. He had some big fucking problems and I should call Bob.

"Okay, Jerry. Here's the program. You put everything on freeze-frame until I get a hold of Bob and the police. I don't want any bodies sliding out any windows into any dumpsters until we sort this out. You clear on this?"

"But the guy is tilted and staring at me," said Jerry.

"Then cover him with a sheet and sit down with the six-pack. Hear me?" Jerry responds, "Well, okay."

Bob Spiel listened to the entire scenario. "Jerry is a complicated individual with probably a few more faults than most human beings but h e provides great criminal intelligence in the world of stolen art. Kev, call the homicide unit and tell Jerry to stay put until I get there."

As I finished up my midnight shift duties, Bob called in to relate that the homicide detectives were satisfied with Jerry's version of the events and after conducting interviews at the bar, were convinced he was telling the truth. The medical report reflected an accidental death due to an overdose of heroin.

Bob said the worst thing that could have happened with Jerry. I h ad to meet Jerry and Bob said, "No problem. I need an alternate Agent in case I'm busy. You're the first Agent other than myself Jerry has ever listened to and followed instructions."

Jerry at the time was in his late fifties but looked like he was in his late seventies. Years of alcohol abuse, drug use, smoking and erratic eating habits had aged him, but, when he wanted to, he could be quite charming.

Jerry Dillion had studied art at the prestigious Art Institute of Chicago and then spent several years in Europe studying the master painters. He returned to Chicago and because of his habits fell in with the wrong crowd. By the time I met him he had spent about one-third of his adult life in jail for non-violent crimes such as fraud and, of course, forgery.

Jerry loved cowboys and Indians so his favorites were the artists whose paintings depicted the American West. He was fond of recreating scenes from the work of those artists, especially Frederic Remington and Charles Russell. He knew all their works by heart and during one of his drinking binges pencil sketched a scene from one of Remington's paintings. This was fine except he then signed it "F. Remington" and sold the small sketch for five-thousand dollars. The gallery owner who purchased it was so impressed that he asked Jerry if he could acquire any more of these rare drawings. When Jerry saw the check he neglected to mention that he, not Remington, had drawn the scene.

A constant flow of information from several sources alerted Bob Spiel that Remington and Russell drawings and paintings were appearing in the Chicago area. Bob checked out the art work and knew they were forgeries. His investigation led to a particular gallery which was making enormous profits from these paintings.

We discussed the situation and decided we would start with a physical surveillance of the gallery and then would determine if there had been a mail fraud violation since the items may have been shipped to the gallery. The third phase of the investigation would be to either develop a source inside the gallery or plant someone inside to observe the operation.

Since the gallery was located on tony North Michigan Avenue, it was a fun surveillance with plenty to look at and minimal threat to the Agents working the case.

It took a few days before Bob and I observed Jerry walking down lovely Michigan Avenue on a picture-perfect day carrying a large rectangular object wrapped in paper. Bob turned to me and said, "Ten to one Jerry is headed for our gallery." I responded, "Do we call this a clue or what!"

Jerry walked into the gallery and after about half an hour walked out. Bob looked at me and said, "Hit it! Lower Wacker Drive. Get off and head to Blackie's on the east side."

Blackie's was a bar located under Michigan Avenue and we parked near it and waited. In about ten minutes we saw Jerry walking down Grand Avenue headed for Blackie's before he could enter the bar we pulled up beside him. "Perhaps we could offer you a ride?" Bob asked. Jerry's reply was, "I've got some people to meet in here. I'll see you guys later."

"Okay, Jerry. I'm not quite as proper as Bob. Get in the fuckin' car or I'm going to throw your ass up against the building, cuff you and then throw your ass in the car," I snapped. "Damn it, Kevin. You could be a little nicer," whined Jerry.

Jerry got in the car. We drove over to Grant Park and went for a walk. Jerry denied everything until we suggested we would be going through all this clothing, which would not be on his body at the time, looking for the cash or check he had just received at the gallery. Jerry kept saying, "Aren't we all friends here?" He wanted to know if he

109

showed us the money could he treat us to drinks at Blackies'? Unlike most of his acquaintances, we declined his generous offer.

We then proceeded to make Jerry a counter-proposal of our own. We told him that, if he agreed to cooperate, we would recommend probation, but only if he would testify truthfully about the gallery owner and his knowledge that the paintings were forgeries. "Jesus, guys. You don't make my life easy. Cut me some slack," he whined. Jerry was agitated and indecisive about his predicament.

In a very calm voice, Bob said in his scholarly way, "Jerry, this is one of those pivotal moments in one's life and, Lord knows, you've had your share. Here are the options. We arrest you for forgery and, reflecting on your prior record, a five-year prison term isn't out of the question. Or, you cooperate, we ask for probation and we move on with our lives here in Chicago." Jerry looked at me with a sheepish grin. "I think Bob is on to something, Jerry," I said.

A few days later, as I opened the door to the interview room at the Chicago FBI Office, "Jerry the Forger" was being creative. The room had been transformed into an art studio. On his canvas were cowboys, buffaloes and Indians. I closed the door and wondered if a forgery had ever been committed inside the confines of an FBI Office before this.

Jerry appeared promptly for "work" every morning at the Chicago Office. It took him about two weeks to produce a beautiful Charles Russell replica. Jerry was the model "worker." He was off the booze and the drugs and focused on his art. It was one of the few times I really saw Jerry enjoy himself and look happy.

The painting completed, we wired Jerry up and drove him to North Michigan Avenue. As we monitored the conversation, Jerry got the owner to acknowledge the painting was like the other twenty Jerry had sold him and that he was aware Jerry had painted it, not Charles Russell. The owner insisted Jerry help him pick out an expensive frame which would up the price at auction. Luckily, the owner overlooked Jerry's comment that this would be the most expensive frame the owner had ever picked out in his life.

The business concluded, Jerry returned to the car shaking. "I'm not used to all that pressure. How do you think it went?" he asked. "Robert DeNiro couldn't have done it better," I answered. Bob chimed in, "Yes. Kudos, Jerry."

At the United States Attorney's Office, the ever efficient Assistant U.S. Attorney Gary Shapiro approved going forward with search and arrest warrants. Federal Judge Marvin Aspen of the Northern District of Illinois approved the warrants and we were in business.

The auction was held the following Saturday. The gallery owner looked out over the hundred or so bidders, a little larger crowd than normal, perhaps because his catalog highlighted a rare Charles Russell painting that had just come on the market. Unknown was the fact that it had come on the market via the FBI. He was unaware of the ten FBI Agents in the crowd with their bidding paddles in hand and their service automatics under their suit jackets. The rest of the bidders were similarly dressed, less the revolvers, and the women were perfectly coifed.

After about forty-five minutes, with two Agents dozing off, the Russell was brought on stage. The bidding started at fifty thousand dollars. The second bidder was Bob Spiel, who waved a federal search warrant. The shaken gallery owner almost collapsed on stage and the bidders let out a collective gasp. The Agents quickly rose from their chairs and ordered everyone to remain seated. It was a great moment in law enforcement! The beautiful people were stunned and shocked that an FBI raid was taking place in this upscale part of town, let alone in an elegant art gallery.

After a few months of negotiations, the owner pleaded guilty and received a hefty fine and jail time. The gallery remains open under the same name but with new ownership and management.

Once the big case was behind us, Jerry needed to renew his driver's license. He asked me to accompany him to the State of Illinois Building since Bob was on vacation.

Now you have to understand that although Jerry the Forger's true name was Jerry Dillion he had operated under several aliases: Jerry Costello, Jerry Abbott (from the comedy team of the nineteen forties and fifties – Abbott and Costello), Jerry Hammond, Jerry Diamond, Jerry Marx (he thought that name was cute because of Karl). I arrived at the driver's license facility to find Jerry in a frenzy.

"What's the matter, Jer?" I asked. "Oh, Kevin, I hate any place that's official—it always reminds me of the joint. And, I lost my license," he moaned. "Well, that's okay. It happens all the time," I tried to calm him.

"No, no. You don't understand," he complained. "I can't remember what alias I used or what date of birth." "Jerry, nothing you do is normal. You complicate life beyond belief! What the hell do you want me to do?" I asked. "Just walk me through the steps," he answered.

Jerry went to the first station and explained he had lost his license and he needed a replacement. The sympathetic employee asked him his name. "Jerry Johnson" he replied. I stared at him in disbelief but said nothing as he provided the rest of the descriptive data.

"Why didn't you just tell him you were Jerry the Forger? That's what everyone else knows you by," I asked. Jerry smiled and said he had just read an article about the coach of the Dallas Cowboys and the name Johnson just came to mind. "Chicago Bears fans will be really happy to hear that," I said.

Shortly after the driver's license escapade, Jerry moved to California. Bob and I thought we had heard the last of him until about a year later when Bob got a call. "It's Jerry. He's still in California." "Great," I said. "Our crime rate will stay down for a little while longer."

"Probably for about another year to be precise," Bob explained. "He's in Lompoc Correctional. Something about 'being framed' for check kiting."

The year passed quietly until a t heft occurred at the University of Chicago. Some rare artifacts from the University's Institute of Egyptology, located on the campus near Chicago's Hyde Park neighborhood, had been stolen. The University of Chicago is world renowned for its Department of Economics in addition to its exceptionally high academic standards. It is also distinguished for its curriculum concerning Egyptian history. The University's epigraphic survey team, based at Chicago House in Luxor, Egypt, is preeminent in its field. Bob Spiel was assigned the case and after we examined the facts we were sure it was an inside job. The question was did the thieves have a private buyer or would they unload the stuff to a dealer?

Just about that time, Jerry surfaced back in Chicago, broke but free. He was very amenable to accepting an assignment. We decided that since Jerry's reputation in Chicago was fairly well known, we would run a reverse sting operation, front him as the buyer and see what happened.

Jerry was to put out the word at antique shops in and around Hyde Park that he was in the market for the type of artifacts that had been stolen from the Institute. Before Jerry started his rounds, he called me. "Kevin, I need to borrow one of your guns." My response was, "Jerry, you're a convicted felon. I'm an FBI Agent. FBI Agents don't lend guns to convicted felons." "But, I'm working for Bob and Hyde Park is a rough area," he explained.

"Look, Jerry," I pointed out, "You're an alcoholic, a drug user, you have dead guys in your bed and you want to dump them out your apartment window. No, I don't think giving you a gun is a good idea." He asked, "Will you come with me? I need some protection."

"Jerry, go there at noon time. Get some mace, a baseball bat, but forget about the gun!"

Jerry made his contacts and a few weeks later got a call. Jerry somehow talked to the shop owner into letting him take the artifacts to have them examined by an expert. The pieces were positively identified as the stolen artifacts. We contacted the shop owner who agreed to cooperate and, since the items had not been transported interstate, notified the Chicago Police Department. A joint investigation identified a secretary at the Institute as the thief. At the last minute University of Chicago officials decided that since the artifacts had been recovered and to avoid the possibility of adverse publicity at a trial, they fired their employee. The case never went to court but the artifacts were returned to their lawful owner.

Things were once again normal—Jerry the Forger was back in Chicago.

CHAPTER NINE

THE PERPETRATOR'S NEGOTIATORS

San Juan,

Puerto Rico

It was during my assignment in San Juan, Puerto Rico, that I began to see the evolution of another role for FBI Special Agents— that of negotiating with criminals. This responsibility has continued to evolve to this day but had its inception with the New York City Police Department. The number of situations in which criminals and police found themselves in a standoff became so prolific that some forward-thinking New York police officers realized the need for a specialized negotiator to talk with the criminal and ultimately resolve the situation in a peaceful fashion. Every time the negotiator responded to a crime scene, he or she increasingly gained insight into the criminal mind. It did not take long before the FBI concluded that this process was beneficial for all of law enforcement. With the assistance of the

New York Police Department, the FBI produced its own "expert negotiator" and marketed the art of negotiating as a subject for police schools across the country.

Special Agents, being the resourceful human beings they are, became quite good at negotiating with criminals and an enormous amount of knowledge gained from experience was gathered on the subject. The FBI has always had the strength to learn from its mistakes and to use those situations as case studies for its police schools. Being able to analyze one's failings so they do not occur again results in a stronger organization.

My first experience with the FBI hostage negotiators occurred at the Chilean Consulate in Puerto Rico. Two Puerto Rican Nationalists had taken over the consulate in Old San Juan at gun point. Their aim was to exchange the Consul General and three other hostages for some Puerto Rican terrorists incarcerated in the United States. This was prior to President Bill Clinton's administration which would have gladly granted clemency without the necessity of taking over the Chilean Consulate.

Two of our Puerto Rican Special Agents negotiated unsuccessfully for fifteen hours straight before the decision was made

119

to assault the consulate. My anti-terrorist team was to rappel down the side of the building from the roof to the fourth floor and enter through the windows. I was across the alley in a parking garage with a grenade launcher with which I was to fire a tear gas projectile to signal the beginning of the assault.

The negotiators were in contact with the two nationalists who were continuing to hold the four hostages in these offices. The plan was for me to fire into the window at 0800 hours. The negotiators made clear to the nationalists that their time was expiring and a decision was needed immediately. At 0759 a call came in that they were surrendering and coming out of the consulate. I switched my launch selector from the "fire" position back to "safe." As I looked down on the alley and watched everyone exit the building, hands raised high, I was aware that our hostage negotiators had saved lives and prevented unnecessary violence from taking place. I was relieved that the power of the word had won out over the power of a gun. I unloaded the grenade launcher, placed the projectile back into my ammo pouch, and proceeded down the driveway of the parking garage, feeling a whole lot better about the beginning of a new day.

Upon my next assignment in Chicago, Illinois, I hooked up with two of the finest hostage negotiators ever to carry the credentials of an FBI Agent—Bob Scigalski, "The Polish Prince," and Jack O'Rourke, "The Monsignor." These two men were experienced, intelligent and totally dedicated to resolving a hostage crisis in a peaceful manner. The Prince and the Monsignor were assigned to C-2, a criminal squad, composed of ten Special Agents, including myself.

Both Agents taught hostage negotiating to police agencies not only in the Midwest but all over the world, and were recognized as experts in the field. While I had not been formally trained at an FBI school, I often accompanied the dynamic duo during their negotiating assignments and collaborated with in the process of resolving crisis.

My first collaboration did not go well. A distraught father was holding his daughter hostage in the hayloft of a barn. When he announced that he was claustrophobic I suggested there was a window at the end of the barn which he could open for air. Bob and Jack agreed it was a good idea and Bob, who had built up a rapport on the phone with the father, mentioned it to him. Seconds later we were all stunned when the father came diving through the window, head first, and fell into a haystack! We looked at each other in astonishment at which time Monsignor O'Rourke commented, "Well, God bless you, Kevin. It worked!" Other agents rescued the hysterical daughter from the loft. Dad was on his way to the hospital to have his cuts taken care of and to undergo a psychiatric evaluation. The Prince, who had been observing all of this activity, still with the phone is his hand, turned and looked at us. "Okay, Agent Man, it's Miller time!" I felt I had bonded with the boys or such a generous invitation would not have been extended.

Now that I was an ex-officio member of this famous negotiating team, I couldn't wait for the next situation to present itself. I didn't have to wait long as about a week later a most unusual occurrence took place. Special Agents had gone out to the northern suburbs of Chicago to arrest a federal parole violator. He had been a fugitive for about a year and his wife was being evicted from their home. The wife had been cooperating with the agents in an effort to locate her fugitive husband. She had called and told the agents that her husband was at the house collecting some of his things. As the agents approached the house, the fugitive spotted them, jumped into his car and fled the area. The wife told the agents that in addition to taking his clothes and his dog, he had picked up a loaded Colt .45 automatic from the bedroom. The agents pursued the fugitive through the suburbs and onto the Kennedy Expressway. The Illinois State Police had been alerted to the fact that the fugitive was driving south on the expressway headed from O'Hare Airport toward downtown Chicago. Illinois State Police units proceeded to get into position and slow the traffic down, closing off-ramps and giving the agents time to close in from behind. This was a Friday evening on a major artery into Chicago. With guns drawn, the troopers and agents approached the vehicle. The fugitive looked around frantically and grabbed his dog, a beautiful brown and white collie. "Back off, coppers, or the dog gets it!" Everyone stared in disbelief—the guy was holing his dog hostage. The standoff was on.

The call came in and at first we thought it was a joke. The State Police Commander made it very clear that there was nothing funny about 1,000 cars a minute backing up on the busiest expressway in the area, at the busiest time of day, on the eve of a weekend, because of one of *our* fugitives. It took about fifteen minutes for the Prince, Monsignor and me, Agent Man, to arrive on the scene. The commander was right—it was not a pretty scene. Thousands of cars, fifteen police units, flashing lights of red and blue, surrounded one small white compact car that contained a white guy, his dog and a damn big automatic.

I looked at the commander and said, "Just shoot him!" "Don't think I haven't considered it," he replied. "The problem is there are tons of civilians whose safety has to be considered. Plus, this is a residential area and right up there, Agent Man, is a school yard with youngsters playing." The commander was absolutely right. This was a no-fire zone, at least for the moment.

Monsignor O'Rourke said, "Commander, with your permission we'd like to talk to Wayne." The commander nodded. Bob asked the fugitive, Wayne, if we could throw him a phone since he had implied that anyone who approached the car would be shot, along with the dog. Wayne agreed to talk. During the next four hours we listened to Wayne's life story—his brushes with the law, his time served in prison, his jobs, mostly part-time, and his return to crime, though not very successfully. He talked about his wife and how he had failed her. When Wayne started to cry, we put Monsignor on the line with his understanding voice and sympathetic ear. When it was time to return to the reality of the hostage situation, the Polish Prince, with his authoritative voice, took the phone.

There was tremendous pressure on us to resolve the predicament. News helicopters hovered overhead and our superiors were indicating that they wanted it wrapped up. We had talked to Wayne about everything under the sun. Bob put him on hold and said, "Guys, I'm out of shit to talk about." Jack grinned, "That's a first. Let me get my tape recorder." We laughed and I said, "How about the dog? He didn't take his wife when he left, he took the dog." Bob lit up. "You're right. We negotiate the release of people, so why not the dog?" Jack nodded in agreement and commented, "Sure, maybe we can exchange it for a dog sled." Wayne got right into the conversation. He told us how much he loved his dog, how loyal it had been, never making value judgments and how the dog was always there for him.

Bob looked at us, "Where do we got with this?" I responded, "Ask him when was the last time the dog ate or drank water." Jack chimed in, "Tell him we'll get the dog food and water. Damn, we'll throw in a kennel if he throws out the gun and surrenders." "Good, Monsignor," I agreed. Then Bob gave him the hard sell and told him that time was up. The Kennedy Expressway could no longer wait for one man or his dog.

At first, Wayne did not respond but, as we watched, the window of the compact rolled down, the automatic came flying out and clanked on to the pavement. The standoff was over and the troopers rushed to get Wayne out of the car and traffic moving again on the Kennedy. As we walked up to the car, Wayne, now in handcuffs, tears in his eyes, pleaded, "Take care of my dog like you promised, will you?" "Yeah, Wayne, he'll probably be treated better than you," I said. An animal control officer took the dog to his truck and we watched the traffic slowly start moving again. Bob said, "Well, my Friday night plans are shot." "Mine, too," I agreed. Jack, with a twinkle in his eye asked, "Anyone for Binyon's Bar?"

The month had passed quickly and we had just returned from firearms training at the Chicago Police Academy when our supervisor walked into the squad room in the Dirksen Federal Building. He announced, "We have a situation at 35th and Drexel." I commented, "What? Urban renewal funds dry up?" The supervisor didn't see the humor and directed us to proceed to the area. Monsignor O'Rourke looked at me and said, "You see, Agent Man, you'll never advance in today's FBI because you've got a sense of humor and in order to get promoted you cannot laugh!" Bob just smiled as we got into our Bureau car.

As we got out of the car I looked across the vacant lot at a large five-story brick building and asked, "Are my eyes deceiving me, or are those gun ports in the side of the building?"

Lt. Terry Hillard, Chicago Police Department, was crouched down behind a nearby car. "You get over here, Agent Man, before you get shot. This is a combat zone!" Terry (now the Superintendent of the Chicago Police Department) is one of several fine Chicago police officers with whom I had the pleasure of working and he was a very street-smart officer. "Welcome to the headquarters of the El Rukn street gang, the most violent gang in the city," Terry said. I looked at him and responded, "If this is by invitation only, my friends and I can leave now." Terry laughed and then explained that his fugitive task force had tracked a federal fugitive to this location. Before they could effect the arrest, he took refuge in the building. The problem was compounded by the fact that there were at least fifteen more heavily armed gang members in the building.

Terry had Chicago Police tactical units and two FBI SWAT teams standing by in case a building entry was necessary. FBI technical agents had already set up a field telephone so we could talk to the occupants. The spokesperson for the El Rukns was a man calling himself "Seeque" who indicated that "Radum," our fugitive, was in the building and was being afforded sanctuary. I turned to Monsignor O'Rourke, "Maybe you can give Seeque a short history of the sanctuary movement." Jack then got on the phone and in his best father-confessor voice explained that we had only one objective—the arrest of Radum—not an invasion of the sanctuary of the El Rukn headquarters. He went on to mention that the building was not recognized as a religious structure and therefore was subject to bombing, demolition and assault by paramilitary forces of the police and the FBI. He pointed out, "The final touch is that you can't make bail if you're removed in a body bag. These bad tidings could all go away if Radum was handed over. You can all go back to drinking Kool-Aid or whatever you all do in the building together."

Seeque indicated they would have to talk it over and he would get back with us. "I think you covered the whole ball of wax, Monsignor. Now let's hope they see it our way or the shit's going to hit the fan," I said after Jack had hung up.

A few minutes later, Seeque called us and said they were willing to give up Radum as long as they were not charged with harboring a fugitive and no attempt was made to enter the headquarters. Jack asked them to send Radum out the front door. Seeque argued, "That would be bad for our image since the whole 'hood is watching and the media have their cameras focused on the building." After consulting with Jack, Bob and I headed down the alley, with our guns drawn, to the back door of the headquarters. In a moment the door opened and Radum was being pushed out the back door with the door being quickly shut behind him. Radum was banging on the door yelling, "Oh, man, let me back in. Is this any way to treat a brother?"

I said, "FBI, Radum. Get your ass over here 'cause they're not going to let you back in!" Bob shouted, "Yeah, get over here now 'cause we're late for choir practice and you're late for your court date." Radum reluctantly, with hands raised, walked over to us. We cuffed him and led him away.

As soon as Jack saw we had cleared the alley, he spoke into the phone. "Seeque, nice doing business with you, my man. Party on!" He abruptly hung up.

129

It had been a busy week after the El Rukn arrest and I had spent most of the week in court testifying in an Interstate Transportation of Stolen Property case. Jack and Bob were downstate in Southern Illinois teaching a police school.

As I walked toward the federal garage I was thinking about dinner with my bride, Pam, and a nice quiet Friday evening. I ran into John "Arson" Larsen, an outstanding Special Agent who was on the fugitive squad but specialized in the investigations of suspicious fires, hence the name. John, too, had plans for the weekend but, as so often happens in the life of an FBI Agent, crime does not take the weekend off. John was headed out to Mannheim Road in a western suburb of Chicago where the police h ad located a bank robbery suspect out of Alabama in a motel. We headed to the motel and learned the fugitive, "Fast Freddie" Langton, was holding his girlfriend hostage. The motel was surrounded and other agents from the fugitive squad were already on the scene. I looked at my watch, knowing that our dinner reservations were for two hours later.

"John, we've got to get this thing off center." I said. John indicated we were in phone contact with Fast Freddie. "You guys have any automatic shoulder weapons with you?" I asked. "Always. H & K 10

130

mm submachine guns. Why do you ask?" "Well, get them out so Fast Freddie can see them." John and the other agents went into their trunks and five submachine guns appeared. Even the on-scene police officers were impressed by the show of firepower.

I took the phone. "Hello. Fast Freddie?" I introduced myself and asked him what type of handgun he had in his possession. Fast Freddie replied, "A mother-fucker .357 Magnum." I inquired, "Is that any different than a regular .357 Magnum? Because if it isn't you better look out the window and see those Special Agents with the submachine guns in their hands!" The curtain was drawn back for an instant and then closed.

"Here's the deal, Freddie. When was the last time you ate!" I asked. "Several hours ago and I could use a Big Mac and a shake about now," he answered.

"Freddie, I don't have time to fuck around with you because you're screwing up my dinner plans. I'll make you a deal. You surrender, bring the girl safely out, and lay down the gun. I'll bring you a Big Mac and a shake before you go downtown. You refuse the offer and I send in the five agents with the machine guns and we scrape you and the girlfriend off the floor. What's it going to be?"

"Don't you guys usually wait out the offender?" asked Freddie.
"Yeah, that's standard operating procedure but we have to change that because I'm under a time constraint. So you have to tell me which part of the deal you want. It's nothing personal but time's up!"

"Okay, but you're not bullshitting me on the Big Mac and shake, are you?"

"No, Freddie, I always deliver. Now put the gun down, send the girl out first, and then you, hands up. The shake and burger will be delivered to your—whoops, I mean *our*—squad car!"

The agents cuffed Fast Freddie and read him his rights. John delivered the food and I headed to dinner with the bride.

CHAPTER TEN

SOMEWHERE OVER CUBA

San Jose,

Costa Rica

The year had been an excellent recruiting season for the Chicago Office of the FBI. I had been assigned to the difficult job of being a regional recruiter covering three states—Illinois, Indiana and Wisconsin—in an effort to find the best and brightest for the position of Special Agent.

My job was made infinitely easier by our outstanding recruiting staff of Leonie Schultz, Donna Furlan and Nanette Skopelja, who would later become a successful Special Agent in the Chicago Office. Leonie and Donna were the senior staffers who answered all the questions and knew how to process candidates with their eyes closed. These three ladies would be responsible for placing the Chicago Office in the number four position out of fifty-eight field divisions for successfully recruiting Special Agents. This was an extraordinary accomplishment when you consider the population centers of the United States.

Knowing that the office was in good hands, I had chosen July to take my vacation and looked forward to two weeks of relaxation in the jungles of Costa Rica. My experiences in Southeast Asia during the Vietnam War had caused me to love the jungle but without getting shot at. I learned to enjoy the beauty of the jungle during my combat tour of duty in Vietnam but decided that traveling through the jungle in Costa Rica without the explosions would really be relaxing. This would be my fourth foray into a rain forest without an enemy trying to annihilate me.

My two favorite people were to accompany me on the trip. My bride of over twenty years, Pam, was used to my exotic destinations, and my son, John, who always welcomes an adventure no matter in what part of the world it is located.

We had flown to Miami from Chicago and were waiting to board American Airlines Flight 989 which would take us non-stop to San Jose, Costa Rica. We had observed four individuals who appeared to be in their thirties, definitely Americans and on vacation, boarding the aircraft. My son, John, remarked, "Dad, I think these guys have spent most of their time in the bar." The four were loud, joking, and basically obnoxious. At this particular moment of boarding they were not offensive or using profanity but their conduct left a lot to be desired. I replied to my son, "They're probably going fishing in Costa Rica, work hard all year, and are just letting their hair down a bit."

We had wanted to sit together and took three seats at the very rear of the aircraft near the galley where the flight crew prepared meals for the passengers. The takeoff went smoothly and we settled down to enjoy the three and one-half hour flight to Central America. I had been in Central America before and always enjoyed the people and the landscape. Most of the countries there are relatively poor but the people are warm, hardworking, and trying to improve their lifestyle.

We had been in the air about an hour when I overheard a conversation one of the flight attendants was having with a co-worker. One of our four obnoxious Americans had made some suggestive comments to her and then rubbed her leg while she was serving beverages. She had warned the passenger that such conduct was not appreciated or tolerated by her company. The man laughed and told his friends that he thought she liked him and they should get together in Costa Rica.

Shortly after that, a second flight attendant returned to the galley and described a similar encounter with another individual in the party. He had touched her breasts and remarked, "Nice set, baby." She was upset and complained to her colleagues, "I don't have to put up with that shit!" The senior flight attendant, Nancy Zalesky, said she would inform the captain of the problem and have him talk to the passengers. After hearing this conversation, I got up, introduced myself and told them what I did for a living, offering any assistance that I could render. Nancy indicated they could handle the problem but was most appreciative of the offer of assistance.

As soon as I sat down my son asked, "What's up, Pop?" I repeated what I had heard and John asked, "So, are you going to go up there and kick their ass?" I laughed and answered, "Not quite yet, son, but if it comes down to that I'll expect my backup man to be ready to go!" John was excited and responded, "Always!" Since he was a football player and weight lifter I felt confident in enlisting his assistance. Although only sixteen years old, he had been in similar situations with me in the past and had always proven to be an asset under any circumstances.

The four men sitting in rows ten and eleven received a visit from Captain Richard Durnan who explained it was a federal offense to interfere with a flight crew attempting to carry out their duties and that he personally did not appreciate their conduct toward the female members of his crew. The men laughed and said they were just kidding but would cause no more problems.

As the flight attendants began serving the meals, the captain announced that off the left side of the aircraft was the island of Cuba. It was a beautiful day and as I looked down out of the window I could see Havana Harbor and the beautiful beaches of the island's south coast. I hoped some day to visit that island and observe its beauty close up.

As I sat back down I noticed one of the flight attendants walking rapidly down the aisle. When she got to the galley she burst into tears, explaining that the passenger in Seat 10-A had propositioned her and grabbed her arm, not letting her continue to serve the other passengers.

The senior flight attendant then got on the phone. After her conversation she walked over to me and said, "Sir, the captain would like to see you up front in the cockpit." I replied, "Certainly."

As I headed up to the front I took special note of the man in Seat 10-A and his companions. None of them appeared to be in top physical shape and their consumption of alcohol had diminished their response time, except when trying to intimidate young flight attendants.

I was let into the cockpit by one of the flight attendants and met Captain Durnan. He indicated he had talked to the men but they must have had short term memories because about thirty minutes after the conversation they were again interfering with his flight crew. "Frankly, Kevin, I'm not quite sure how to handle this. Any suggestions?" "Well, Captain," I asked "how far out from San Jose are we?" "We're about one hour from wheels down," he answered.

"Okay, my suggestion would be to radio the San Jose tower, explain the problem briefly, and ask that a security group of at least six meet us upon arrival. In the meantime I'll go back in the cabin and have a chat with those nasty boys." Captain Durnan then said, "Kevin, don't put yourself at risk. I don't want to escalate this situation."

"Captain, I do this for a living and if we get to the point where we need to tie these assholes up, then we'll do that." "Okay! Just be careful."

I returned to my seat to tell Pam and John what had transpired. John asked, "Dad, do you want me to come with you?" "No, John, but if you see a couple guys roll into the aisle, I'd appreciate a little help." "You bet. I'll be all over that place!" I situated John in the aisle seat so he could observe rows ten and eleven and come forward should the situation require it.

I then advised the senior flight attendant of what I had in mind. I also asked her to try to find some type of restraining devices in case things did not go well. She immediately went to the galley and produced several pairs of flexicuffs which were used to secure electrical wires and dining carts during emergencies. I indicated that she should have those available should I need them. "Not a problem," she said and added, "Actually, it would be a pleasure." The phone rang and she answered it. The arrangements had been made in San Jose and a security contingent would meet the plane upon arrival. I glanced at my watch. It was fifty-one minutes until touchdown.

I looked at Nancy and said, "Showtime!" She smiled and laughed.

When I arrived at row ten I noticed that the middle seats in both row ten and eleven were vacant.

"Hi, boys. How are you all going?" The passenger in 10-A looked up and said, "Who the fuck are you?" I looked down at him and excused myself as I sat down in the middle seat. I stared into his blood-shot eyes and said, "I'm Kevin Illia from the FBI and you boys have not been acting like gentlemen. What's your name?" The man answered, "I'm Ray and I'm an attorney and you don't scare me, agent man, because you have no jurisdiction on an international flight over Cuban airspace. So fuck off."

"Well, Ray, I could have guessed you're an attorney by your arrogant behavior. But, you must have slept through that class in law school that dealt with international law or you would know that a nation's sovereignty extends to its national carriers. See, Ray, if we were on Cubana Airlines with a lot of little Fidels running through the cabin, you would be absolutely right. But, since we're on American Airlines over Cuban airspace, I think you and your friends have a problem." He looked into my face and his eyes widened as the lights inside went on. "What's the issue, agent?" "Well, here's the deal, Ray. You pissed off the captain not once but twice. You see, his girls aren't hookers, they're flight attendants and while they're very attractive, they don't like being groped by you and your friends." I turned to the two men in row eleven and asked, "Are you boys with me so far? Are you catching the gist of this conversation?" There was a two-word reply from row eleven. "Yes, sir."

Suddenly Ray and his friend, Glenn, were focused in on what I was relating to them. Glenn offered a question, "What's this mean, sir?" "Well, first of all it's Kevin, not 'sir.' And secondly, Glenn, it means that in less than an hour when we arrive at San Jose you'll have a reception committee to meet you."

Ray protested, "Does that mean we're being arrested? Because we haven't committed a crime! This is absurd and silly plus the Costa Ricans can't charge us for anything on an American carrier. Right?"

"Ray, you're a lot sharper than you led me to believe," I replied. "Let's review the situation. You interfere with the flight crew, you're warned by the aircraft commander and you ignore his warnings. Then you tell me I have no jurisdiction and then tell me that the country in which you're landing, Costa Rica, has no jurisdiction. Let me guess, you boys have never been to Central America before and you have no idea how many bananas we buy from these people each year. That

141

gives us tremendous leverage when we make a request. Tell me the truth, Ray, do you think these people give a shit what you're charged with. They love the fact that you're foreigners, especially Americans, who are being branded bad Americans!"

"I've had enough of this shit. I want to see the captain and then someone from the American Embassy!" Ray shouted. "Cool down, Ray, or I'll have to cuff you like a common felon. The American Embassy! Boy, that'll really piss these guys off if you start out like that. They might just put you up against the wall and shoot you!"

Ray had a blank expression on his face and Glenn was staring at his hands. A voice from the back row asked, "They don't really do that anymore, do they?" As I looked back and to either side of me, four sets of eyes were glued on me. "Here's the deal, boys. This thing is out of proportion. I'll try in my humble capacity to intervene on your behalf. I don't know what's going to happen. You may end up in one of those Spanish dungeons but I don't think they'll put you up against the wall. Although I do recall one time in the D.R., Dominican Republic......Oh, that's not important." There was complete silence until Ray finally asked, "Kevin, will you help us?" "Gee, Ray, five minutes ago you were telling me to fuck off." Glenn interrupted, "No, no, Kevin, he's a smart ass. Please help us!"

"Well, okay. No mention of embassies or ambassadors. When the Costa Ricans come, it's 'yes sir' and 'no sir.' When leaving the plane, an apology to the flight crew, especially the captain, and no matter what happens, no swearing or mouthing off. Got it?" 'Yeah, yeah," Ray and Glenn responded.

"You guys in the back hear that?" "Yes, sir, we're with you!"

Just then the announcement came on that we were arriving in San Jose. The four Americans were sober and in no mood to interfere with any more flight attendants.

As we taxied up to the gate the captain told everyone to keep their seats as Costa Rican officials were boarding the aircraft. I looked out the window and saw a blue and white police van with flashing blue lights on top accompanying the plane to the gate. I heard Ray mutter to himself, "Holy shit, we're fucked."

As the plane came to a stop I remarked, "You boys stay here. I'm going up front, and don't move." The door opened and in front of me was a gentleman in tie and white shirt accompanied by six uniformed police officers armed with automatic sidearms and Uzi submachine guns. I thought to myself, "They take this stuff seriously. If we'd been at O'Hare Airport in Chicago, the Chicago police would have sent out one uniformed officer with a .38 revolver."

"Buenos tardes. Soy Kevin Illia del FBI," I introduced myself. The gentleman in the white shirt smiled and in perfect English responded, "Señor Illia, I am Rafael Sanchez of the Costa Rican Airport Security Detail. You requested our help?" "Yes, sir. Basically we have four drunk Americans who took a liking to the flight attendants and could not keep their hands off them."

"What would you like us to do?" I replied, "I think detain them for a while and scare the shit out of them." I guess *detain* is a word that is open to interpretation because Rafael responded, "I can keep them for a week, a month, or put them in an old Spanish prison, which they will not like."

"I think they're already familiar with the Spanish prison there. I think just an interview room and some questions will do," I answered.

I ducked back into the plane and motioned the group forward toward the exit. They got their belongings and in a somber mood walked down the aisle apologizing to everyone, including the flight attendants and the captain.

When they saw Rafael and his unit they all greeted him with, "Good afternoon, sir." Rafael regarded them with a cold stare and said, "This way!"

The two-hour interview ended with a Costa Rican security official warning them about their conduct during their five-day fishing trip and destroying their return flight tickets. Ray, who had become a most humble spokesman for the group, inquired how they were supposed to leave the country without airline tickets.

The security official looked at him for a moment and said, "Señor, that is your problem but you had better be gone before sunset."

I thanked Rafael and his men for their assistance, posed for pictures since reruns of the "FBI" television show were big in Costa Rica, which made me an instant celebrity, and then departed.

The four detainees thanked me for saving them from the dreaded wall and as I walked out the front of the airport my two favorite pals were sitting on our luggage with big smiles on their faces.

"Vacation, anyone?" I asked. Pam answered, "One can always hope, Agent Man!" John looked at me and started laughing.

Kevin R. Illia

ABOUT THE AUTHOR

Born in San Francisco, Kevin Illia spent four years in the United States Air Force, with a combat tour in Vietnam. He then attended Sonoma State University in California and later earned his graduate degree from Washington University in St. Louis.

Appointed a Special Agent of the FBI in 1971, Mr. Illia spent the next 24 years earning the nickname "Superman", investigating bank robberies, kidnappings, and extortions, leading an anti-terrorist team on the island of Puerto Rico, and concluded his career in Chicago investigating organized crime and public corruption.

In recent years he has served as a Court Administrator and Special Investigator for the Office of the Chief Judge of the Circuit Court of Cook County.